Orient BlackSwan Abridged Texts

GULLIVER'S TRAVELS

Jonathan Swift

Abridged by
V. Gopalan Nair

Edited by
Seetha Srinivasan

Orient BlackSwan

Acknowledgements

The publishers and the editors have written to Palgrave Macmillan for 'Gulliver's Voyage to the Houyhnhnms' by Kathleen Williams from *Swift: Modern Judgements* (1968). Though no reply has been received at the time of going to press, due and appropriate acknowledgement will be made in all future editions of this book. As for '*Gulliver's Travels*' by Maynard Mack from *Swift: A Collection of Critical Essays* (Prentice Hall, 1967), every attempt is being made to trace current copyright holders and since no information has been made available at the time of going to press, efforts will be continued and due acknowledgements will be made in all future editions of the book.

ORIENT BLACKSWAN PRIVATE LIMITED

Registered Office
3-6-752, Himayatnagar, Hyderabad 500 029 (A.P.), India
e-mail: centraloffice@orientblackswan.com

Other Offices
Bangalore, Bhopal, Bhubaneshwar, Chennai,
Ernakulam, Guwahati, Hyderabad, Jaipur, Kolkata,
Lucknow, Mumbai, New Delhi, Patna

First Published 2010
Reprinted 2012, 2013, 2014

ISBN: 978 81 250 4011 8

Typeset in Warnock Pro 10.5/12.5 *by*
OSDATA, Hyderabad 500 029

Printed in India at
Aditya Offset Process (I) Pvt. Ltd.
Hyderabad

Published by
Orient Blackswan Private Limited
3-6-752, Himayatnagar, Hyderabad 500 029 (A.P.), India
e-mail: hyderabad@orientblackswan.com

Contents

Introduction

Life of Jonathan Swift

Jonathan Swift was born in Dublin in 1667. Though his parents were of English origin, Swift loved the land of his birth and fought for the Irish cause with great loyalty. England had invaded Ireland and conquered it. Land had been taken away from the Irish and Irish economy was at the mercy of the English aristocracy who engorged themselves and left their Irish tenants in a state of miserable poverty and starvation. It was this state of affairs that prompted Swift to write a fierce satire on the English landlord in *A Modest Proposal.* In this pamphlet, he recommends with ironic seriousness, that every Irish woman should produce children for the Englishman's table. Irony is a literary device by which an author uses words or expressions which mean more or less the exact opposite of what he intends to convey. Their very contrariness is intended to shock the reader, while highlighting their real meaning. Swift exposed the pathetic state of the Irish peasants whose only solution to poverty would be able to sell their children as delicacies for the English nobleman's table.

After his graduation from Trinity College, Dublin, Swift went to London as private secretary to his affluent uncle, Sir William Temple, a politician with some literary pretensions. Temple had written an essay on the comparative merits of Ancient and Modern Learning, a subject of fierce controversy in French academic circles. Temple, who was no erudite scholar had made some uncritical references to certain ancient writers. This invited a very learned but sarcastic retort from Richard Bentley, the librarian of St James library and reputed to be a great scholar of his time. Swift, as a dependent and relative of Temple felt that he should vindicate his patron and punish his opponent. The result was the famous prose satire *Battle of the Books*, written in the mock-heroic style to ridicule Bentley's retort. The book assumes that an epic battle (as between the Greeks and the Trojans) is being fought between the books in St James library divided into two opposing parties—the Ancients and the Moderns. The elaborate machinery of the epics is employed to mock this meaningless controversy.

Swift took the holy orders and was ordained a priest of the Anglican Church. He wrote a witty allegory on the religious controversies of the time entitled *A Tale of a Tub*. An allegory is a literary device which consists of the use of symbol to express a deeper philosophic meaning. Serious ideas are symbolically conveyed through a simple fable or parable. *A Tale of a Tub* is a celebrated satire on the corruptions in religion conveyed through a simple story of three brothers, Peter, Martin and Jack who allegorically represent the Catholics, Anglicans and Non-conformists or Calvinists respectively. Swift holds up for acceptance the Anglican faith. His light-hearted treatment of religious matters so horrified Queen Anne that his prospects of Church preferments where permanently endangered. He remained the Dean of St Patrick's Cathedral in Dublin to the end of his life, and this thwarted ambition sometimes led to a gloomy cynicism.

Although Swift was cynical about women and sceptical of human relationships, a biographical study reveals his deep attachment to two young women, Esther Johnson and Esther Vanhomrigh addressed by him as Stella and Venessa. His private correspondence with Esther Johnson, published as a *Journal to Stella* reveals the depth of his affection and the warmth and humour of Swift the man.

Swift's greatest literary work is *Gulliver's Travels* published in 1726. Although Swift professed to hate the species called 'man,' he loved individuals. *Gulliver's Travels*, apart from its great merit as a classic for children, is a satire on human nature. Though Swift posed as a cynic and a misanthrope and his satire was harsh and bitter, he was steadfast in his concern for humanity and was honest as a critic.

Swift died in 1745. Most early literary criticism, rumour and a great number of Swift's own statements, quoted only in part and occasionally even distorted, point to the theory of Swift's increasing insanity since middle-age and to the fact that he was stark mad at the time of his death. Prof. Irvin Ehrenpreis in a brilliant study of the author's life and his works *The Personality of Jonathan Swift* (1962) sums up all modern literary and medical evidence to refute the theory of his madness: "Swift from birth to death was insane by no medical definition. He was no more eccentric or neurotic than Pope or Johnson, and probably less so. The tradition of his madness has been rejected for forty years by every qualified scholar who has bothered to look into the question."

The twentieth-century approach to Swift is different. We have come a long way from the judgements of his contemporaries who criticised his works, especially *Gulliver's Travels*, as the angry outpourings of an embittered lunatic and misanthrope, repulsive, obscene and unfit to read. It is important to understand that it was Swift's excessive concern for humanity, his despair at humanity's ever-increasing pride that made his satire harsh. If Swift was pessimistic about people and was a misanthrope – he would never have written *Gulliver's Travels*. Like all great satires, the principle aim of *Gulliver's Travels* is to instruct and correct through ridicule, irony and sarcasm. The book exposes with great intensity the ugliness of human nature, the vices of conceit, pride and cruelty, but the underlying tone is consistently one of compassion—a desire to instruct humanity and put them on the right path of Christianity.

Structure and Plot of the Novel

Gulliver's Travels was the culmination of Swift's literary achievement—his magnum opus. It was begun in 1720 and finally published in 1726. It is at once a delightful, fantastic story of adventure for children, a political allegory, and a serious satire on human nature, on contemporary politics, social institutions, religious controversies and on the manners and morals of the age. The book is written in the form of a travelogue. The hero and narrator of the story is Lemuel Gulliver, an English physician who opts to travel as a ship's surgeon when he is unable to take care of his family on his meagre income. Gulliver is endowed with a keen, almost journalistic sense of reportage, and a desire to travel. The book is made up of four parts, each dealing with the persona's experiences in a different fantasy land.

Part I, A Voyage to Lilliput, deals with Gulliver's experiences in the land of the little people, who are no more than six inches tall. It is on one level an absorbing tale of the adventures of the giant Gulliver among the Lilliputians and on another level rich in allegorical references to the politics in England. It is above all a scathing satire on the moral pettiness of humans as seen in the behaviour of the Lilliputians. Human beings are filled with the sense of their own grandeur and importance, and cannot view themselves with objectivity. Their pride and boastfulness are revealed as ridiculous when perceived from Gulliver's great height.

Gulliver escapes from Lilliput and returns to England. Before long he sets out on a second voyage which takes him to Brobdingnag. In Part II, A Voyage to Brobdingnag, the situation is reversed. Gulliver is now marooned and dwarfed in the land of giants who are over forty feet tall. He now becomes the midget he had laughed at in Lilliput. Observed through the microscopic eyes of Gulliver, the Brobdingnagians are hideous in size and stature, and Gulliver realises that he must have been just as hideous to the little people in Lilliput. Here, Swift satirises the physical grossness of the human and the grotesque ugliness of the human body.

The malignancy of the human as a political animal and the accompanying propensity for destruction are portrayed in the person of Gulliver. He is little more than an insect in Brobdingnag and at his best, an amusing toy. His glorious account of the English political system and England's preparations for war horrify the benevolent Brobdingnagian king who in a tirade on mankind concludes that the English must be "the most pernicious race of little odious vermin that Nature ever suffered to crawl upon the surface of the earth" (149).

Gulliver ends up in a miniature box which is picked up by a giant eagle and dropped into the ocean. This signals his departure from Brobdingnag and the beginning of his voyage to Laputa.

Part III, A Voyage to Laputa, Balnibarbi, Luggnagg, Glubbdubdrib and Japan, is a satire on the scientists and philosophers of the age. The people of Laputa have extraordinary physical features, heads turned at an angle, one eye turned upward and the other inward. The Laputans, we are told, are so taken up with 'intense speculation' about theoretical mathematics that they constantly worry about abstract issues such as the sun burning out or a comet colliding with the earth. But they are totally inept when it comes to practical things like constructing straight walls for their houses. Through the people of Laputa, Swift ridicules the experiments of the Royal Society and allied institutions of the time. His descriptions of the projects at the Academy of Lagado are brilliantly comic and emphasise their impractical nature. For example, one of the architects in the Academy experimented with building houses, starting at the roof and working down to the foundations. Glubbdubdrib is the island of sorcerers and magicians where it is possible to summon people who are dead to make an appearance. Gulliver amuses himself by summoning Homer and Aristotle and comparing them and others. In Luggnagg, Gulliver encounters the strange phenomenon of the Struldbruggs, immortal beings with decay in their bones and "deformities in extreme old age"(231) attending them. The experiments at Laputa, Balnibarbi and Luggnagg do not yield anything—they result only in misery, decay and death. The frightening emptiness and sterility of a purely scientific society (without religion) is evident from this book. After a brief journey to Japan, Gulliver returns to England before setting out on his final voyage to the land of the Houyhnhnms.

Part IV, A Voyage to the Country of the Houyhnhnms, narrates the experiences of Gulliver in the land of the Houyhnhnms or horses, and the Yahoos. These horses are creatures governed solely by reason, free from any emotion or passions, while the Yahoos who physically resemble human beings are ruled purely by 'animal' instincts. The human is placed between the two extremes of rationality and animality. Observed from the Houyhnhnm viewpoint, Gulliver or 'man' whom the eighteenth century had defined as an animal whose most striking feature was the ability to reason, is primarily a Yahoo, with only a glimmer of reason. Gulliver is repulsed at being identified with the Yahoos in the land of the Houyhnhnms. In his conversation with the master-horse (whose language Gulliver has learnt) he explains the customs practised in England, including the wearing of clothes by humans (who resemble the Yahoos), the government of the people, the legal system, and the uses of money as instruments of purchase. Many of the concepts cannot be translated into the Houyhnhnm language as their vocabulary and range of experience were limited. The horses with their total lack of feeling and emotion are seen as being far from ideal. They are as dull and insipid as the Yahoos with their animal sensuality are revolting. Swift seems to indicate to us that the nature of the human is complex and defies definition unlike that of the Yahoos and the Houyhnhnms. The book for all its harsh satire and anger, instructs humans to see themselves with humility and honesty; it condemns pride, ego and myopic self-esteem. It urges every person to use reason to be a good Christian.

Gulliver finds himself in looks, speech, and manner becoming more and more like the Houyhnhnms. He grows content living with his Houyhnhnm master and hopes to be as like them as possible. However, fortune does not favour him and it is decreed that he must leave the land for he is after all a Yahoo to the Houyhnhnms. Gulliver returns to England but has difficulty adjusting to life with his family after such extraordinary and bizarre adventures.

Important Themes and Motifs

1. The Theme of Travel and Discovery

The travelogue, a popular genre of writing in the eighteenth century, chronicles the experiences and adventures of a traveller. It is generally written from the first-person point of view giving immediacy to the experiences narrated. It is also a literary genre which the author manipulates to suit his purposes in the text. *Gulliver's Travels* is a fictional travelogue containing factual elements related to travel by sea.

The four Parts of *Gulliver's Travels* are linked by the theme of travel and discovery. Each of the parts starts off with a voyage leading to a destination. However, the voyage only works as a means to get to a place of adventure. The travails he suffers en route such as being shipwrecked or captured by pirates serve as reasons for him to abandon the sea and find new lands. Each of the islands Gulliver arrives at offers varying and diverse experiences for the traveller. The entire novel is contained within the framework of a travelogue documenting the new, bizarre, and occasionally life-threatening experiences that befall Gulliver.

It is important to note that in the case of Swift, the form of the travelogue is a vehicle for expressing his deeper and more vital concerns which are related to inherent human follies, foibles and weaknesses. Travel and discovery offer opportunities to present Gulliver in varied situations where the pride and depravity commonly associated with the human race are exposed and he is made to see himself and his fellow beings in a more realistic light, with all their limitations and shortcomings.

A travelogue takes the reader on a journey along with the traveller in the narration, discovering places and observing the customs and manners of the people through the eyes (perspective) of the writer-narrator. Eighteenth century travelogues include Samuel Johnson's *A Journey to the Western Islands* (1775) and Laurence Sterne's *A Sentimental Journey through France and Italy* (1768). A modern travel narrative, *The Middle Passage* (V. S. Naipaul) takes the reader through the Caribbean islands, informing with irony and humour the customs and traditions of the people. What is distinct about Swift's travelogue is that it is entirely fictional and borders on fantasy. The places that

Swift describes and Gulliver visits: Lilliput, Brobdingnag, Laputa, and the land of the Houyhnhnms belong to the realm of fantasy and are figments of Swift's imagination.

The first voyage takes Gulliver in the direction of the West Indies and ends up in a shipwreck. Tossed about in a little boat and thrown into the sea, Gulliver finds himself on the island of Lilliput. He wakes up from an exhausted sleep and encounters the people of the island who are not more than six inches tall. Gulliver's description of the people takes into account their language and expressions as well as details of the food and drink served to him. The inhabitants of the island, we are told, are excellent mathematicians and enjoyed the patronage of the Emperor. A carriage is constructed to transport Gulliver half a mile into town where he is housed in an ancient temple. Gulliver wins the favour of the Emperor and his Court and the people in general as he learns their language and extends a hand of friendship to them hoping to gain liberty in return. Gulliver is given his liberty and asked to serve the emperor in the battle with Blefuscu.

The second voyage begins in the ship called *Adventure.* Gulliver, in the company of the sailors, arrives at the Cape of Good Hope where he stays for some time before setting sail again. After passing the straits of Madagascar, they sight land and arrive at Brobdingnag. Swift's narrative conforms to the structure of the travelogue as the reader is given a description of the land of Brobdingnag—from the grass which is twenty feet tall, corn stalks forty feet high to the men and women who are veritable giants. Each stride takes the giants ten yards ahead. The sound of their voices is compared to thunder and the rush of a watermill. Gulliver joins the farmer's family for a meal at the dining table, thirty feet high where he stumbles over a crust of bread and falls headlong on the table. Here again Gulliver begins to learn the language of the giants and communicates his needs to his hosts.

Gulliver is treated as a curiosity and paraded in a box on market-day. He is taken to the metropolis called Lorbrulgrud where he is displayed ten times a day "to the wonder and satisfaction of all people" (116). Finally the attention of the King and Queen are drawn to this diminutive creature who resembles a human being and Gulliver entertains them as well. Gulliver is also given an opportunity to inform his curious host about life in England, the political Parties, the Parliament, and the judicial system. But the King is not impressed and when Gulliver explains the use of gunpowder and offers to manufacture it for the King, the latter concludes that Gulliver and his race are malicious beings intent on harming fellow humans for the slightest cause. Gulliver's voyage to Brobdingnag ends when he is carried off along with his box by a large bird and then dropped into the sea to be rescued by a passing ship.

The voyage to Laputa in the ship *Hope-well* starts off badly when the ship is seized by pirates. Gulliver is set adrift in a canoe which takes him to a group of islands. The flying island of Laputa is described together with the curious inhabitants, the Laputans. The preoccupations of the Grand Academy of Lagado provide comic relief. Swift's attempt is to make each of the voyages as full of fantasy as possible. Everything is exaggerated for satiric effect—nothing bears resemblance to normal life as it is lived in England. The worlds that Gulliver inadvertently stumbles into are filled with strange sights and people, far removed from what he has hitherto experienced in the land of his birth and each subsequent place he visits.

The references to new lands and new discoveries echo the growing interest in the study of science in the eighteenth century which was also the Age of Enlightenment or the Age of Scepticism. The great scientist Sir Isaac Newton had propounded new scientific theories and it was beginning to be believed that science would open doors to an explanation of the mystery called life. This resulted in an ever-increasing scepticism towards religion which was now equated with blind faith. Probably Gulliver's discovery of Laputa points to this change of perspective that was happening in Swift's times.

Glubbdubdrib is described as the Island of Sorcerers or Magicians where, through the power of necromancy, the dead ancients could be summoned for a period of twenty four hours each. The island of Luggnagg is distinguished by the Immortals or Struldbruggs who bore a red spot on the forehead distinguishing them from the rest of the populace. Although immortal, they are not immortally youthful and often lament that the peace of death is denied to them.

The final voyage takes Gulliver to the land of the Houyhnhnms and Yahoos, where the former looked like horses but were guided by reason in thought and action, while the latter were sensual and disgusting creatures who resembled humans. There is a sharp contrast between realism and fantasy in Gulliver's experiences in each of the islands. The 1726 edition of the novel bears the title *Travels into Several Remote Nations of the World, in four parts by Lemuel Gulliver,* giving the impression that it is yet another travelogue recounting significant details of discovery of new and unexplored territories.

2. As a Satire of Human Nature

Satire is a literary genre in which human vices, weaknesses, foibles and follies are held up to ridicule. Wit and humour are commonly used as instruments of satire. Satirical writings were popular in England in the eighteenth century. Some of the well-known satires of the period include Pope's *The Rape of the Lock*, Mandeville's *Fable of the Bees* and Swift's *A Modest Proposal* and *Battle of the Books* which range from gentle to biting satire. Reason and virtue were concepts central to the eighteenth century philosophical discourse. While writers like Shaftesbury saw the human as 'naturally' benevolent and endowed with virtue, others like Swift perceived a disconnect between moral standards set by society and actual ways of living. In *Gulliver's Travels*, Swift uses satire as a vehicle to point to the depraved state of humankind. Some critics have observed that Swift is a misanthrope because he paints human nature as a whole in a sordid and gloomy light, almost as if there are no redeeming features to humanity. Others see Swift's work as an attempt to jolt the human race out of its complacency, and turn them towards the direction of self-realisation and redemption. Swift seems to be holding up a mirror to society so that in viewing the gross magnification of its vices, humanity has a hope for the future. Describing Swift's satirical technique, Basil Willey comments: "His effort is always to strip the object satirized of the film of familiarity which normally reconciles us to it, and to make us see it as in itself it really is, as the child saw the unclothed emperor in Hans Andersen's story." (*The Eighteenth-Century Background*. Harmondsworth: Penguin Books, 1965. pp. 105.).

The voyages to Lilliput and Brobdingnag focus on the flaws in human society, with particular reference to English society. In Lilliput, humans are seen as diminutive creatures, crawling about without dignity or grandeur. Their efforts and institutions are devoid of significance and they seem to wallow in empty pride. The situation is reversed in the next part where humans are observed as physically coarse, vulgar and gross in Brobdingnag. Gulliver's grand presentation of the nature of English political and judicial institutions is met with a caustic remark from the King on the pernicious nature of the human being which reflects Swift's own stance regarding the hollow and contemptible nature of British legal and political systems. The King is only Swift's own vehicle of truth.

The satire on human nature becomes more pointed and sustained in the third and fourth voyages. The Laputans are criticised for their preoccupation with speculative reasoning and theoretical abstractions– that the sun may burn up one day, that the earth may collide with a comet and lead to total annihilation. They are not concerned with the practical aspects of everyday living. The projects undertaken by the members of the Grand Academy of Lagado lend themselves to sharp humour and satire. The experiments range from extracting sunbeams out of cucumbers to separating human excrement and reducing it to its original food, and building houses starting at the roof and working down to the foundations. Reason devoid of common sense is satirised in this section. The ludicrous nature of experimentation for the sake of experimentation and having no basis in reality is highlighted here.

In the land of the Houyhnhnms, the roles of humans and animals are reversed. The horses (the Houyhnhnms) represent reason in all its perfection but they have no individual identity. They appear to be the ideal human in the stoicism they maintain but have no human qualities such as compassion or love. They are an unreachable ideal. On the other hand the Yahoos who resemble humans are despicable, sensual, and bestial. Gulliver's voyages conclude with humorous satire as Gulliver is so taken up with the "noble Houyhnhnms" and is so impressed with their culture and their attitudes that he even imitates their gait and manner, trotting and neighing like a horse.

Satire in *Gulliver's Travels* also extends to human institutions, to politics and the state. This will be examined in the section on *Gulliver's Travels* as a political allegory.

3. As Utopian/Dystopian fiction

The term 'utopia' has come to be synonymous with an ideal world or an ideal society. It was first used by Thomas More in his work *Utopia (*1516) where he set out the vision of an ideal society. Plato's *Republic* is also considered a model of an ideal community. Being an ideal, the utopian community is perforce an imaginary one, far removed from the imperfections and inadequacies of normal everyday life. In an utopian society the community holds privilege over the individual and conformity is an imperative. Dystopia was conceived of as the opposite of utopia, and obviously describing an unpleasant, nightmarish world.

Recent works of fiction such as Margaret Atwood's *The Handmaid's Tale* and Octavia Butler's *Dawn* are representations of dystopian fiction. Both utopias and dystopias are usually used as vehicles for satire, exaggerating and highlighting aspects of human nature and behaviour in order to bring about certain necessary reforms.

Gulliver's Travels can be read from the perspective of utopian/dystopian fiction as Lemuel Gulliver journeys from one imaginary island community to another. He examines the social and political structures in Lilliput, Brobdingnag, Laputa, and in the land of the Houyhnhnms. It serves Swift's satirical purpose that the communities are far from ideal and given to excesses of every kind. The land of the Houyhnhnms seems almost utopian but here again, Swift exposes a world where Reason prevails in its perfection but is devoid of individuality or personal identity and therefore leaves much to be desired.

Lilliput is populated by little people who are scarcely distinguishable from one another. They rush about in large groups and crowds performing their tasks as one person. They form a mass of humanity, with no distinguishing features, at least from Gulliver's perspective. The Emperor is different only in that he is a 'nail's breadth' taller, with an Austrian lip, arched nose, and olive complexion.

The Laputan community in Part III is a dystopia which relies on its island-subjects living below it for sustenance. The people of the floating island are peculiarly shaped and clothed and they carry with them 'flappers' to aid their communication with each other. The scientists of their great Academy of Lagado are engaged in pointless experiments, some of which are carried out in the land below slowly leading it to ruin. The new lands Gulliver visits in his third voyage are even more nightmarish because it becomes evident to him that among the "polite and generous people" (224) there lived a bunch of immortals called Struldbruggs who represented living death. Gulliver describes them as the "most mortifying sight"—"Besides the usual deformities in extreme old age, they acquired an additional ghastliness in proportion to their number of years, which is not to be described." (231)

The country of the Houyhnhnms comes closest to being an utopia but still falls short of it. The horses or Houyhnhnms are the masters, described by Gulliver as "orderly and rational", "acute and judicious" (244). Their whole purpose in life is to cultivate Reason and be governed by it. Friendship and benevolence came naturally to the

Houyhnhnms who also practised decency and civility, temperance, and industry. The servants of the Houyhnhnms, on the other hand, are the detestable Yahoos (resembling humans), described by Gulliver as 'abominable' creatures, brutal and despised. Gulliver is so taken up with the "virtues of the inimitable Houyhnhnms" that he has great difficulty adjusting with his family and his life in England when he returns there. He feels alienated there and spends most of his time with the horses in his stable because they resemble his former masters.

It is interesting to note that in Gulliver's description of England, its people, and institutions, England too emerges as a dystopia, an unpleasant, violent, brutal and corrupt society which does not practise what it preaches.

4. Gulliver's Travels as a Political Allegory

An allegory is a literary genre (in prose or verse) which is structured in such a way that its meaning could be read on two levels – a primary or literal level, and a secondary and more complex level. An allegory is defined as a narrative in which the characters, plot, setting and occasion, while making sense in themselves also signify a second layer of meaning where they point at another set of people, events and setting either from the writer's social milieu or recent historical events. It is a figurative mode of representation where ideas are conveyed through symbolism and metaphor. Swift uses satire to highlight the allegorical elements in his tale and thus the allegory functions as an excellent vehicle of criticism of the English government and its activities. The allegory and the satire, in a sense, are interwoven inextricably and deftly.

Many readers familiar with eighteenth century politics of England see in the book a revision of those events. Hence it is often studied as a political or historical allegory; the characters and action are based on historical or political personages and events. Allegories work as a critical interpretative frame and in historical and political allegories, characters and actions in the text represent people and events in real life. For instance, John Bunyan's *Pilgrim's Progress* is a moral or religious allegory that presents the Christian philosophy of salvation through suffering. *Gulliver's Travels* is a political allegory in which the text contains symbolic references to actual people and events in eighteenth century England. Allegory and satire are closely intertwined, one form serving the other.

There are several allegorical references to life in the Royal Court of George I (who came to the throne in 1714) in the first section of the novel. The flippancy and hollowness of court life are satirised through the Lilliputian ministers and their antics. Sir Robert Walpole seems to be presented in the person of Flimnap the Treasurer while Skyresh Bolgolam has been identified as possibly, the Earl of Nottingham. The punishment decreed for Gulliver, namely of putting out his eyes and starving him instead of putting him to death at once is curiously reminiscent of the Crown's decree on Lord Bolingbroke and the Earl of Oxford. They were accused of high misdemeanour instead of high treason and hence escaped the death penalty, for the sentence only entailed a loss of their titles and estates. Lilliput's hostility towards and the battle with Blefuscu brings to mind the antagonism between England and France at the time. The Whig and Tory Parties presented in the text as Tramecksan and Slamecksan are differentiated by the height of their heels, thus trivialising the principles they stood for. Religious disputes and theological arguments between the Roman Catholic and the Anglican Churches are lampooned in the form of the conflict between the Big-Endians and the Little-Endians.

The late seventeenth century was also the age of scientific enquiry and religious scepticism. Charles II was a patron of the arts and sciences. In 1662 he established the Royal Society which carried out scientific experiments and encouraged the growth of other branches of learning. In the Grand Academy of Lagado and its outlandish experiments, Swift found an avenue for satirising the Royal Society, its experiments and publications. The scholars and philosophers of Laputa were so concerned with theoretical abstractions that the practical aspects of everyday living were completely overlooked. Laputa is an allegorical representation of the developments with regard to science in the century. The experiments in the Academy of Lagado and those practised in the lands below such as building a house from its roof downwards and the modern methods of cultivation only leave the general populace miserable and the country ruined. This does not, however, stop the scientists from continuing with their experiments.

As a political allegory of European civilisation, Swift presents the aspects of war and the European propensity for destruction, particularly in the parallels that one can draw between Lilliput's desire to enslave an already defeated Blefescu and the strained relationship between

England and France. He also indirectly criticises the arrogance of European imperialists who 'civilised' through brutality and oppression while masking their chief motive which was greed. Patterns of war and destruction are woven into the allegorical motif here to explicate the existing political situation that Swift is satirising.

Gulliver as a Character

Characters are central to the plot of any story, and especially longer fiction. They are influenced by the events in the story just as the events are structured by characters. Characterisation is defined as the art of creating characters which seem close to real life and have a role to play in the development of the novel. The author's fictional world can be populated by 'flesh and blood' characters with recognisable human qualities, or they can be 'stock characters,' that is, mask-like and representing particular ideas that the author has. E M Forster uses the terms 'flat characters' and 'round characters' to show this distinction. A 'flat character' is often a type, a static, two-dimensional character, without much individuality, or even development. A 'round character' on the other hand is dynamic, three-dimensional, and exhibits a certain degree of complexity. Such a character 'grows' in the course of the novel and is even capable of surprising the reader.

It is a little difficult to talk of Gulliver as a full-fledged character in *Gulliver's Travels*. He is closer to being Swift's mouthpiece or the 'persona' in the novel rather than a full character in his own right. A 'persona' refers to a first person narrator, the 'I' of the narrative. It is Gulliver who narrates his experiences throughout the four Parts of the novel. His narrative voice cannot be confused with the perspectives of the author, although there is a certain overlapping particularly in Part IV.

Gulliver offers a personal introduction of himself, his family, and the circumstances surrounding his becoming a ship's surgeon and a world traveller. In his encounter with the Lilliputians in Part I, he tries to give the reader as many details about the place and its people as possible. He attempts to reproduce the language and expressions used by the Lilliputians – 'Hekinah Degul,' 'Tolgo phonac,' 'Langro Dehul,' and 'Peplom Selan,' among others. This makes his account more realistic and convincing. By means of detailed descriptions Gulliver creates the illusion of size – a giant amidst an ant-like population.

Everything is seen through Gulliver's eyes and perceived through his interpretation of events. He informs the readers of his gentleness and good conduct, and how he cultivated a favourable disposition among the people of Lilliput. In spite of this we are told that Skyresh Bolgolam and Flimnap the High Treasurer are moved by jealousy and envy and schemed against him. Gulliver takes credit for his resourcefulness which enabled him to escape disaster and return home to England.

Gulliver as a character is restless for adventure and new experiences. The second voyage to Brobdingnag is a reversal of the experiences at Lilliput. Gulliver creates the illusion of reality through visual and palpable details such as the farmer's enormous dinner table which dwarfed him, the huge dish of meat, the cup which held two gallons of drink, and the rock-sized crust of bread which he tripped over and fell flat on his face. Gulliver's comments help the reader to understand his character, its growth and development or perhaps degradation as the case may be, especially in the light of the last part of the book. Comparing the oversized women of Brobdingnag with English women, Gulliver observes that the fair skins of English women appear beautiful only because their counterparts are of the same size and are not scrutinized under a magnifying glass to reveal the rough coarseness of their skin. Gulliver's growing disgust with the human body begins here and later multiplies after his stay in the land of the Houyhnhnms.

The farmer's nine-year-old daughter whom Gulliver calls Glumdalclitch takes him under her wing, tutors him in the Brobdingnagian language, and rescues him from accidents on account of his miniature size. Glumdalclitch is described as being a "dexterous at her needle and skilful in dressing her baby" (111). The characters in the novel are closer to caricatures, exaggerated in shape, size, and other physical and mental attributes. There is no dialogue marked to reveal character in some way. Most of the speeches are lengthy monologues which merge into the narrative.

In Laputa, Gulliver feels marginalised as the Laputans were interested only in mathematics and music, both of which left Gulliver behind in competence. On his visit to the Grand Academy of Lagado, Gulliver is sceptical of the experiments conducted there. Each experiment is more bizarre and useless than the other, and far removed from practical life. On his acquaintance with the Struldbruggs he arrives at the conclusion that death was far better than the "living death" that the Struldbruggs represented.

Gulliver informs the reader that after each voyage he found his wife and children in good health. He does not give us any other details concerning his personal life in England. There is no description of the emotion that accompanies reunion or feelings of nostalgia at being away from home. His patriotic feelings which are aroused when his country and her deeds are abused by the Brobdingnagian King slowly wane till he himself is vociferously critical of England by the time he reaches the land of the rational horses. For instance in Part II, he talks at length about the judiciary:

> I then descended to the Courts of Justice, over which the Judges, those venerable sages and interpreters of the law, presided, for determining the disputed rights and the properties of men, as well as for the punishment of vice, and protection of innocence (145).

This changes by the time Gulliver reaches the land of the Houyhnhnms when he describes the same judicial system as follows:

> . . . these Judges are persons appointed to decide all controversies of property, as well as for the trial of criminals, and picked out from the most dexterous lawyers who are grown old or lazy, and having been biased all their lives against truth and equity, lie under such a fatal necessity of favouring fraud, perjury, and oppression, that I have known several of them refuse a large bribe from the side where justice lay, rather than injure the *Faculty* by doing anything unbecoming their nature or their office (267).

Gulliver's disgust with England and its government extends to the entire human race and it is in Part IV that the reader is convinced that Gulliver is Swift's mouthpiece. This is evident in the way he derides and satirises English society and its institutions. Gulliver is fed, and housed by the horse-like Houyhnhnms who become his masters. He is full of admiration for this superior race which is intelligent and orderly, as well as rational. They represent to him the model of an ideal society. He despises the Yahoos who personify vile humanity to the extent that he recoils at the embrace of even his wife when he goes back to England.

At the end of *Gulliver's Travels*, it is difficult to say if Gulliver is an eighteenth century allegorical figure or a rounded and complex character. His growth and development in the course of the narrative is restricted to the change in his attitude towards his fellow human beings although he arrives at some kind of self-awareness towards the end of the text, the awareness being that he is a Yahoo! Critics have also doubted the reliability of Gulliver's narrative – is it satirical from beginning to end, or does Gulliver himself become the object of satire in Swift's hands? Like Christian in Bunyan's *Pilgrim's Progress*, Gulliver might also be an allegorical representation of humanity in general.

Significant Techniques and Aspects of Style

The significant elements of style in *Gulliver's Travels* can be studied under the headings of narrative style, imagery, the language of satire, and the use of irony.

1. Narrative Style

The book employs the first-person point of view and the voice is that of a traveller reporting and documenting his personal experiences. Each of the four voyages begins with a departure from an English port and ends with a return to England. It is a linear narrative taking the reader on a journey of discovery which includes a critical reflection on English society as well as its institutions. The book opens with a personal introduction of Gulliver, the third of five siblings, a student of Emmanuel College, Cambridge, surgeon's apprentice, and eager traveller. Gulliver learns navigation and other aspects of instrumentation that would equip a traveller setting out on sea voyages.

Realism as an approach to fiction was only just becoming familiar to readers in the eighteenth century. Swift's approach in *Gulliver's Travels* is a combination of the realistic and the fantastic. While realism seems an attempt to give the narrative credibility, the realistic elements which involve England, his childhood and family serve as anchors for they bring Gulliver back after every adventure and provide the setting for a new voyage. They also imply that Gulliver does not go looking for fantasy lands; rather his journeys are primarily to feed his family and to keep them in comfort. It is right to say in his favour that he does not willingly visit these places but is either ship-wrecked, set adrift by pirates, left by his companions or in the case of the last voyage, the victim of a mutiny. The fantasy worlds of Lilliput, Brobdingnag, Laputa, and the land of the Houyhnhnms are described as if they really existed and could be reached by a traveller. In fact, after almost every journey, Gulliver brings back curiosities or riches that he sells for a high price.

However, prominence is given to what he sees, hears and experiences in the lands he finds himself in. Events are reported as seen through the eyes of Gulliver and speech is presented in the form of long monologues which merge with the narrative. It is also a point of interest that the narrative although not dated every day almost resembles the style in which a log book of a ship or a travelogue is kept. Events seem to be recorded as they occur although it is clear that they could only have been put to paper on his return after every journey or at the end of all his journeys. It is therefore safe to assume that the account is not entirely in a 'factual' mode, for events are narrated from memory, which to use a Rushdiean trope, has been 'pickled' for long years and may not be what it originally was. Realism and fantasy blend doubly in Gulliver's narrative as the fantasy is not just confined to the lands he visits but in his descriptions of the lands themselves for time has served in pickling memories and possibly casting them anew.

2. Imagery

Imagery and motifs are literary devices or elements that the author introduces in the text to describe and give life to the narrative. Images are also used for the sake of symbolism. The overt preoccupation with human filth and excrement is a deliberate attempt to draw the reader's attention to the coarseness and baseness of the human body and its functions. In Lilliput, Gulliver urinates in 'torrents' much to the amazement of the people crowding around him; the scientists in Lagado recycle excrement and the Yahoos drop excrement from trees. The cure for the Yahoos' diseases is "a mixture of their own dung and urine" (281) which is forced down their throats. Gulliver suggests during the visit to Brobdingnag that even the most beautiful of human forms would appear ugly and coarse when seen at close quarters, or seen enlarged as through a magnifying glass. The eighteenth century preoccupation with the nobility of the human soul is contrasted here with the vulgarity of the human condition. In Part IV, Gulliver is described as a 'brute animal', while the horses become superior beings.

The imagery of size is used in *Gulliver's Travels* to draw attention to misplaced human pride and the fact that power and self-importance depend entirely on circumstances and are not inherent in human nature. Gulliver, who feels he is a giant among diminutive creatures in Lilliput, is regarded as ridiculously puny in Brobdingnag. The Queen in Brobdingnag is surprised at "so much wit and good sense in so diminutive an animal" (119). On hearing from Gulliver of the uses of gunpowder, the King is "amazed how so impotent and groveling an insect as I could entertain such inhuman ideas" (151).

3. Language of Satire and Irony

Gulliver's Travels is described by critics as a scathing attack (satire) on humanity's depraved condition. Irony and satire are tools used by the writer to jolt his readers into an awareness of the evil inherent in humans, and thereby bring about change. The voyage to Brobdingnag contains several instances of Swift's satire on the moral nature of man. Chapter 7 of Part II (the chapter bearing the title 'Gulliver's Proposal is Rejected') is an example of the creative use of satire. In this chapter, the author satirises England, human inhumanity to fellow beings, and the human sense of self-importance while attempting to praise them. It is a tongue-in-cheek presentation of facts pertinent to the narrative. Swift's satire is more direct and pointed in the chapter that describes the projects of the Grand Academy of Lagado. The choice of projects and the seriousness with which they are undertaken contribute to the ridiculousness of the ventures and the total picture of life in the island of Laputa. Satire has the further function of drawing a parallel between the fantasy world being satirised and the real world of the author. In this case the satire and allegory are directed at England and English institutions.

Irony and satire are used liberally and forcefully in Part IV as lawyers are described as "proving by words multiplied for the purpose, that white is black, and black is white, according as they are paid" (267). Gulliver ends with a catalogue of occupations available to English people as a result of society's injustice and man's greed and immorality – "begging, robbing, stealing, cheating, pimping, forswearing, . . . fawning, hectoring, voting, scribbling, stargazing . . . libeling, free-thinking . . ." (270). The Yahoos who resemble humans are objects of satire and ridicule in chapter 5 of Part IV– they are "deformed in body and mischievous in disposition" (281). Ironically, Gulliver identifies himself with the Houyhnhnms to the extent that on return to England, human society fills him with "hatred, disgust, and contempt" (309). The human is an "odious animal," a Yahoo after all!

Note: All references to the text of *Gulliver's Travels* are from Rupa Classics (New Delhi: 2010).

PART I: A VOYAGE TO LILLIPUT

CHAPTER ONE: GULLIVER A PRISONER IN LILLIPUT

My father had a small estate in Nottinghamshire. I was the third of five sons. He sent me to Emmanuel College in Cambridge at fourteen years, and I applied myself close to my studies. But the charge of maintaining me (although I had a very scanty allowance), being too great for a narrow fortune, I was bound apprentice to Mr James Bates, an eminent surgeon in London, with whom I continued four years. My father now and then sending me small sums of money, I laid them out in learning navigation and other parts of the mathematics useful to those who intend to travel, as I always believed it would be some time or other my fortune to do. When I left Mr Bates, I studied physic at Leyden two years and seven months, knowing it would be useful in long voyages.

Soon after my return from Leyden, I was recommended by my good master Mr Bates, to be surgeon to the *Swallow* making a voyage or two. When I came back, I resolved to settle in London, to which Mr Bates encouraged me, and by him I was recommended to several patients. I took part of a small house in the Old Jury, and being advised to alter my condition, I married Mrs Mary Burton, second daughter to Mr Edmond Burton, hosier in Newgate Street.

But, my good master Bates dying in two years after, and I having few friends, my business began to fail, for my conscience would not suffer me to imitate the bad practice of too many among my brethren. Therefore, I determined again to go to sea. I was surgeon successively in two ships and made several voyages for six years to the East and West Indies, by which I got some addition to my fortune. My hours of leisure I spent in reading the best authors ancient and modern, and when I was ashore, in observing the manners and disposition of the people as well as learning their language, wherein I had great facility by the strength of my memory.

The last of the voyages not proving very fortunate, I grew weary of the sea and intended to stay at home with my wife and family. After three years' expectation that things would mend, I accepted an advantageous offer from Captain William Prichard, master of the *Antelope*, who was making a voyage to the South Sea. We set sail from Bristol, May 4th, 1699.

In our passage from thence to the West Indies, we were driven by a violent storm to the north-west of Van Diemen's Land. On the fifth of November, the seamen spied a rock but the wind was so strong, that we were driven directly upon it, and immediately split. Six of the crew, of whom I was one, having let down the boat into the sea, rowed till we were able to work no longer. We therefore trusted ourselves to the mercy of the waves, and in about half an hour the boat was overset. What became of my companions in the boat, as well as of those who escaped on the rock, or were left in the vessel, I cannot tell, but conclude they were all lost. For my own part, I swam as fortune directed me and was pushed forward by wind and tide. I often let my legs drop and could feel no bottom. But when I was almost gone and able to struggle no longer, I found myself within my depth and by this time the storm was much abated. I got to the shore about eight o'clock in the evening. I then advanced forward near half a mile, but could not discover any sign of houses or inhabitants. I was extremely tired and I found myself much inclined to sleep. I lay down on the grass and slept sounder than ever, and as I reckoned, above nine hours, for when I awoke, it was daylight.

I attempted to rise but was not able to stir. For as I happened to lie on my back, I found my arms and legs were strongly fastened on each side to the ground, and my hair which was long and thick, tied down in the same manner. I likewise felt several slender ligatures across my body, from my armpits to my thighs. I heard a confused noise about me, but in the posture I lay, could see nothing except the sky. In a little time I felt something alive moving on my left leg; when bending my eyes downwards as much as I could, I perceived it to be a human creature not six inches high, with a bow and arrow in his hands and a quiver at his back. In the meantime, I felt at least forty more of the same kind (as I conjectured), following the first.

I was in the utmost astonishment, and roared so loud, that they all ran back in a fright. Some of them, as I was afterwards told, were hurt with the falls they got by leaping from my sides upon the ground. However, they soon returned and one of them cried out in a shrill, but distinct voice: *Hekinah Degul.* The others repeated the same words several times, but I then knew not what they meant.

I lay all this while in great uneasiness. At length, struggling to get close, I a little loosened the strings. But the creatures ran off a second time before I could seize them, whereupon there was a great shout in a very shrill accent. After it ceased, I heard one of them cry aloud *Tolgo Phonac.* In an instant I felt above an hundred arrows discharged on my left hand, which pricked me like so many needles. They shot another flight into the air, as we do bombs in Europe, whereof many, I suppose, fell on my body (though I felt them not). When this shower of arrows was over, I fell a-groaning with grief and pain, and then striving again to get loose, they discharged another volley larger than the first. Some of them attempted with spears to stick me in the sides. But by good luck, I had on me a buff jerkin which they could not pierce.

I thought it the most prudent method to lie still. My design was to continue so till night, when my left hand being already loose, I could easily free myself. As for the inhabitants, I had reason to believe I might be a match for the greatest armies they could bring against me, if they were all of the same size that I saw.

But fortune disposed otherwise of me. When the people observed I was quiet, they discharged no more arrows. But by the noise I heard, I knew their numbers increased. I heard a knocking for above an hour, like that of people at work. Turning my head that way, I saw a stage erected about a foot and a half from the ground, capable of holding four of the inhabitants with two or three ladders to mount it. One of them, who seemed to be a person of quality, made me a long speech, whereof I understood not one syllable. But before the principal person began his oration, he cried out three times *Langro Dehul san.* Whereupon immediately about fifty of the inhabitants came and cut the strings that fastened the left side of my head, which gave me the liberty of turning it to the right and of observing the person and gesture of him that was to speak. He acted every part of an orator and I could observe many periods of threatenings and others of promises, pity and kindness. I answered in a few words, but in the most submissive manner.

Having not eaten a morsel for some hours before I left the ship, I found the demands of nature so strong upon me, that I could not forbear showing my impatience by putting my finger frequently on my mouth to signify that I wanted food. The *Hurgo* (for so they call a great Lord, as I afterwards learnt) understood me very well. He descended from the stage and commanded that several ladders should be applied to my sides. Above a hundred of the inhabitants mounted and walked towards my mouth, laden with baskets full of meat which had been sent thither by the King's orders. I observed there was the flesh of several animals but could not distinguish them by the taste. I ate them by two or three at a mouthful and took three loaves at a time, about the bigness of musket bullets. They supplied me as fast as they could, showing a thousand marks of wonder and astonishment at my bulk and appetite. I then made another sign that I wanted drink. They slung up with great dexterity one of their largest hogsheads. I drank it off at a draught, for it did not hold half a pint and tasted like a small wine of Burgundy, but much more delicious. They brought me a second hogshead which I drank in the same manner and made signs for more, but they had none to give me.

When I had performed these wonders, they shouted for joy and danced upon my breast, repeating several times as they did at first, *Hekinah Degul*. They made me a sign that I should throw down the two hogsheads, but first warned the people below to stand out of the way, crying aloud *Borach Mivola*. When they saw the vessels in the air, there was a universal shout of *Hekinah Degul*. I confess I was often tempted while they were passing backwards and forwards on my body, to seize forty or fifty of the first that came in my reach and dash them against the ground. However, in my thoughts I could not sufficiently wonder at the intrepidity of these diminutive mortals, who did venture to mount and walk upon my body, while one of my hands was at liberty, without trembling at the very sight of so prodigious a creature as I must appear to them.

After some time, when they observed that I made no more demands for meat, there appeared before me a person of high rank from His Imperial Majesty. Producing his credentials under the signet royal, he spoke about ten minutes with a kind of determinate resolution. I answered in few words, but to no purpose and made a sign with my hand that was loose, to signify that I desired my liberty. It appeared that he understood me well enough, for he shook his head by way of disapprobation, and held his hand in a posture to show that I must be carried as a prisoner. However, he made other signs to let me understand that I should have meat and drink enough and very good treatment. Whereupon I once more thought of attempting to break my bonds, but again, when I felt the smart of their arrows upon my face and hands which were all in blisters, many of the darts still sticking in them, and observing likewise that the number of my enemies increased, I gave tokens to let them know that they might do with me what they pleased.

Upon this the *Hurgo* and his train withdrew with much civility and cheerful countenances. Soon after, I heard a general shout with frequent repetitions of the words *Peplom Selan*. I felt great numbers of the people on my left side relaxing the cords to such a degree, that I was able to turn upon my right and to ease myself with making water, which I very plentifully did to the great astonishment of the people. Conjecturing by my motions what I was going to do, they immediately opened to the right and left on that side to avoid the torrent which fell with such noise and violence from me. But before this, they had daubed my face and both my hands with a sort of ointment very pleasant to the smell, which in a few minutes removed all the smart of their arrows. These circumstances, added to the refreshment I had received by their victuals and drink which were very nourishing, disposed me to sleep. I slept about eight hours, as I was afterwards assured and it was no wonder—the physicians, by the Emperor's order, had mingled a sleepy potion in the hogsheads of wine.

These people are most excellent mathematicians and arrived to a great perfection in mechanics by the countenance and encouragement of the Emperor who is a renowned patron of learning. Five hundred carpenters and engineers were immediately set at work to prepare the greatest engine they had. It was a frame of wood raised three inches from the ground, about seven foot long and four wide, moving on twenty two wheels. The shout I heard was upon the arrival of this engine. It was brought parallel to me as I lay. But the principal difficulty was to raise and place me in this vehicle. Eighty poles, each one foot high, were erected for this purpose and very strong cords of the bigness of packthread were fastened by hooks to many bandages which the workmen had wound round my neck, my hands, my body and my legs. Nine hundred of the strongest men were employed to draw up these cords by many pulleys fastened on the poles. Thus, in less than three hours, I was raised and slung into the engine and there tied fast. All this I was told, for while the whole operation was performing, I lay in a profound sleep, by the force of the soporific medicine infused into my liquor. Fifteen hundred of the Emperor's largest horses, each about four inches and a half high, were employed to draw me towards the metropolis which was half a mile distant.

About four hours after we began our journey, I awoke by a very ridiculous accident. The carriage being stopped a while to adjust something that was out of order, two or three of the young natives had the curiosity to see how I looked when I was asleep. They climbed up into the engine and advancing very softly to my face, one of them, an officer in the guards, put the sharp end of his half-pike a good way up into my left nostril. It tickled my nose like a straw and made me sneeze violently, whereupon they stole off unperceived and it was three weeks before I knew the cause of my awaking so suddenly.

We made a long march the remaining part of that day and rested at night with five hundred guards on each side of me, half with torches and half with bows and arrows, ready to shoot me if I should offer to stir. The next morning at sunrise we continued our march and arrived within two hundred yards of the city gates about noon. The Emperor and all his court came out to meet us, but his great officers would by no means suffer His Majesty to endanger his person by mounting on my body.

At the place where the carriage stopped there stood an ancient temple, esteemed to be the largest in the whole kingdom. Having been polluted some years before by an unnatural murder, it was looked on as profane and all the ornaments and furniture carried away. In this edifice, it was determined, I should lodge. The great gate fronting to the north was about four foot high and almost two foot wide through which I could easily creep. On each side of the gate was a small window not above six inches from the ground. Into that on the left side, the king's smiths conveyed fourscore and eleven chains, like those that hang on a lady's watch in Europe, and almost as large, which were locked to my left leg with six and thirty padlocks. At twenty foot distance, there was a turret at least five foot high. Here the Emperor ascended with many principal lords of his court, to have an opportunity of viewing me, as I was told, for I could not see them.

It was reckoned that above an hundred thousand inhabitants came out of the town upon the same errand. In spite of my guards, I believe there could not be fewer than ten thousand, at several times, who mounted upon my body by the help of ladders. But a proclamation was soon issued to forbid it upon pain of death.

When the workmen found it was impossible for me to break loose, they cut all the strings that bound me, whereupon I rose up with as melancholy a disposition as ever I had in my life. But the noise and astonishment of the people at seeing me rise and walk are not to be expressed. The chains that held my left leg were about two yards long and gave me not only the liberty of walking backward and forwards in a semicircle, but, being fixed within four inches of the gate, allowed me to creep in and lie at my full length in the temple.

CHAPTER TWO

GULLIVER'S POCKETS ARE SEARCHED

When I found myself on my feet, I looked about me, and must confess I never beheld a more entertaining prospect. The country around appeared like a continued garden, and the enclosed fields, which were generally forty foot square, resembled so many beds of flowers. These fields were intermingled with woods and the tallest trees, as I could judge, appeared to be seven foot high. I viewed the town on my left hand, which looked like the painted scene of a city in a theatre.

The Emperor was advancing on horseback towards me, which must have cost him dear; for the beast, although very well trained, yet wholly unused to such a sight which appeared as if a mountain moved before him, reared up on his hind feet: but that prince, who is an excellent horseman, kept his seat, till his attendants ran in, and held the bridle, while His Majesty had time to dismount. When he alighted, he surveyed me round with great admiration, but kept beyond the length of my chain. He ordered his cooks and butlers, who were already prepared, to give me victuals and drink, which they pushed forward in some sort of vehicles upon wheels till I could reach them. I took these vehicles, and soon emptied them all; twenty of them were filled with meat, and ten with liquor; each of the former afforded me two or three good mouthfuls, and I emptied the liquor of ten vessels, which was contained in earthen vials, into one vehicle, drinking it off at a draught, and so I did with the rest. The Empress, and young princes of the blood, of both sexes, attended by many ladies, sat at some distance in their chairs; but upon the accident that happened to the Emperor's horse, they alighted, and came near his person, which I am now going to describe.

He is taller by almost the breadth of my nail, than any of his court, which alone is enough to strike an awe into the beholders. His features are strong and masculine with an Austrian lip and arched nose, his complexion olive, his countenance erect, his body and limbs well proportioned, all his motions graceful, and his deportment majestic. He was then past his prime, being twenty-eight years and three quarters old, of which he had reigned about seven, in great felicity. His dress was very plain and simple, the fashion of it between the Asiatic and the European; but he had on his head a light helmet of gold, adorned with jewels, and a plume on the crest. He held his sword drawn in his hand, to defend himself, if I should happen to break loose; it was almost three inches long, the hilt and scabbard were gold, enriched with diamonds. His voice was shrill, but very clear and articulate, and I could distinctly hear it when I stood up.

His Imperial Majesty spoke often to me, and I returned answers, but neither of us could understand a syllable. There were several of his priests and lawyers present who were commanded to address themselves to me, and I spoke to them in as many languages as I had the least smattering of, but all to no purpose.

After about two hours the Court retired, and I was left with a strong guard, to prevent the impertinence, and probably the malice of the rabble who were very impatient to crowd about me as near as they durst, and some of them had the impudence to shoot their arrows at me as I sat on the ground by the door of my house, whereof one very narrowly missed my left eye. But the colonel ordered six of the ringleaders to be seized, and thought no punishment so proper as to deliver them bound into my hands. I took them all in my right hand, put five of them into my coat-pocket, and as to the sixth, I made a countenance as if I would eat him alive. The poor man squalled terribly and the colonel and his officers were in much pain, especially when they saw me take out my penknife; but I soon put them out of fear, for, looking mildly and immediately cutting the strings he was bound with, I set him gently on the ground and away he ran; I treated the rest in the same manner, taking them one by one out of my pocket, and I observed both the soldiers and people were highly obliged at this mark of my clemency which was represented very much to my advantage at Court.

In the meantime, the Emperor held frequent councils to debate what course should be taken with me; and I was afterwards assured by a particular friend, a person of great quality, that the Court was under many difficulties concerning me. They apprehended my breaking loose, that my diet would be very expensive, and might cause a famine. Sometimes they determined to starve me, or at least to shoot me in the face and hands with poisoned arrows, which would soon dispatch me: but again they considered, that the stench of so large a carcass might produce a plague in the metropolis, and probably spread through the whole kingdom.

In the midst of these consultations, several officers of the army went to the door of the great council-chamber and two of them being admitted, gave an account of my behaviour to the six criminals above-mentioned, which made so favourable an impression in the breast of His Majesty and the whole Board in my behalf, that an Imperial Commission was issued out, obliging all the villages nine hundred yards round the city, to deliver in every morning, six beeves, forty sheep, and other victuals for my sustenance; together with a proportionable quantity of bread, and wine and other liquors—for the due payment of which, his Majesty gave assignments upon his Treasury. For this Prince lives chiefly upon his own demesnes, seldom except upon great occasions raising any subsidies upon his subjects who are bound to attend him in his wars at their own expense. An establishment was also made of six hundred persons to be my domestics, who had board-wages allowed for their maintenance, and tents built for them very conveniently on each side of my door. It was likewise ordered, that three hundred tailors should make me a suit of clothes after the fashion of the country: that six of His Majesty's greatest scholars should be employed to instruct me in their language: and lastly, that the Emperor's horses and those of the nobility and troops of guards, should be exercised in my sight to accustom themselves to me.

All these orders were duly put in execution, and in about three weeks I made a great progress in learning their language; during which time, the Emperor frequently honoured me with his visits, and was pleased to assist my masters in teaching me. We began already to converse together in some sort; and the first words I learnt were to express my desire that he would please to give me my liberty, which I everyday repeated on my knees. His answer, as I could apprehend, was that this must be a work of time, not to be thought on without the advice of his Council, and that first I must swear a peace with him and his kingdom. However, that I should be used with all kindness, he advised me to acquire, by my patience and discreet behaviour, the good opinion of himself and his subjects.

He desired I would not take it ill, if he gave orders to certain proper officers to search me, for probably I might carry about me several weapons, which must needs be dangerous things if they answered the bulk of so prodigious a person. I said, His Majesty should be satisfied, for I was ready to strip myself and turn up my pockets before him. This I delivered part in words, and part in signs. He replied that by the laws of the kingdom I must be searched by two of his officers; that he knew this could not be done without my consent and assistance; that he had so good an opinion of my generosity and justice as to trust their persons in my hands: that whatever they took from me should be returned when I left the country, or paid for at the rate which I would set upon them. I took up the two officers in my hands, put them first into my coat-pockets, and then into every other pocket about me, except my two fobs, and another secret pocket which I had no mind should be searched, wherein I had some little necessaries of no consequence to any but myself. In one of my fobs there was a silver watch, and in the other a small quantity of gold in a purse. These gentlemen, having pen, ink and paper about them, made an exact inventory of everything they saw; and when they had done, desired I would set them down, that they might deliver it to the Emperor. When this inventory was read over to the Emperor, he directed me to deliver up the several particulars.

I had, as I before observed, one private pocket which escaped their search, wherein there was a pair of spectacles (which I sometimes use for the weakness of mine eyes), a pocket perspective, and several other little conveniences; which being of no consequence to the Emperor, I did not think myself bound in honour to discover, and I apprehended they might be lost or spoiled if I ventured them out of my possession.

CHAPTER THREE

THE DIVERSIONS IN THE COURT OF LILLIPUT

My gentleness and good behaviour had gained so far on the Emperor and His Court, and indeed upon the army and people in general, that I began to conceive hopes of getting my liberty in a short time. I took all possible methods to cultivate this favourable disposition. The natives came by degrees to be less apprehensive of any danger from me. I would sometimes lie down, and let five or six of them dance on my hand. And at last the boys and girls would venture to come and play at hide and seek in my hair. I had now made a good progress in understanding and speaking their language. The Emperor had a mind one day to entertain me with several of the country shows, wherein they exceed all nations I have known, both for dexterity and magnificence. I was diverted with none so much as that of the rope-dancers, performed upon a slender white thread, extended about two foot and twelve inches from the ground.

This diversion is only practised by those persons who are candidates for great employments and high favour at Court. They are trained in this art from their youth and are not always of noble birth, or liberal education. When a great office is vacant either by death or disgrace, five or six of those candidates petition the Emperor to entertain His Majesty and the Court with a dance on the rope, and whoever jumps the highest without falling, succeeds in the office. Very often the Chief Ministers themselves are commanded to show their skill, and to convince the Emperor that they have not lost their faculty. Flimnap, the Treasurer, is allowed to cut a caper on the strait rope, at least an inch higher than any other lord in the whole Empire.

These diversions are often attended with fatal accidents, whereof great numbers are on record. I myself have seen two or three candidates break a limb. But the danger is much greater when the Ministers themselves are commanded to show their dexterity; for by contending to excel themselves and their fellows, they strain so far, that there is hardly one of them who hath not received a fall, and some of them two or three. I was assured that a year or two before my arrival, Flimnap would have infallibly broken his neck if one of the King's cushions that accidentally lay on the ground, had not weakened the force of his fall.

There is likewise another diversion, which is only shown before the Emperor and Empress and first Minister, upon particular occasions. The Emperor lays on a table three fine silken threads six inches long. One is blue, the other red, and the third green. These threads are proposed as prizes for those persons whom the Emperor hath a mind to distinguish by a peculiar mark of this favour. The ceremony is performed in His Majesty's great chamber of State, where the candidates are to undergo a trial of dexterity very different from the former, and such as I have not observed the least resemblance of in any other country of the old or the new world. The Emperor holds a stick in his hands, both ends parallel to the horizon, while the candidates advancing one by one, sometimes, leap over the stick, sometimes creep under it backwards and forwards several times, according as the stick is advanced or depressed. Sometimes the Emperor holds one end of the stick and his first Minister the other; sometimes the Minister has it entirely to himself. Whoever performs his part with most agility and holds out the longest in leaping and creeping, is rewarded with the blue coloured silk; the red is given to the next, and the green to the third, which they all wear wound twice about the middle; and you see few great persons about this Court who are not adorned with one of these girdles.

I had sent so many memorials and petitions for my liberty, that His Majesty at length mentioned the matter, first in the Cabinet, and then in a full Council; where it was opposed by none except Skyresh Bolgolam, who was pleased, without any provocation, to be my mortal enemy. But it was carried against him by the whole Board, and confirmed by the Emperor. That Minister was very much in his master's confidence, and a person well versed in affairs, but of a morose and sour complexion. However, he was at length persuaded to comply, but prevailed that the articles and conditions upon which I should be set free, and to which I must swear, should be drawn up by himself. These articles were brought to me by Skyresh Bolgolam in person, attended by several persons of distinction. After they were read, I was demanded to swear to the performance of them; first in the manner of my own country, and afterwards in the method prescribed by their laws.

I swore and subscribed to these articles with great cheerfulness although some of them were not so honourable as I could have wished; which proceeded wholly from the malice of Skyresh Bolgolam. My chains were immediately unlocked, and I was at full liberty. The Emperor himself, in person, did me the honour to be by at the whole ceremony. I made my acknowledgements by prostrating myself at His Majesty's feet; but he commanded me to rise and after many gracious expressions, he added that he hoped I should prove a useful servant, and well deserve all the favours he had already conferred upon me, or might do for the future.

CHAPTER FOUR

GULLIVER OFFERS TO SERVE THE EMPEROR WITH HIS WARS

The first request I made after I had obtained my liberty, was that I might have licence to see Mildendo, the metropolis; which the Emperor easily granted me, but with a special charge to do no hurt, either to the inhabitants, or their houses. The people had notice by proclamation of my design to visit the town. The wall which encompassed it is two foot and an half high, and at least eleven inches broad, so that a coach and horses may be driven very safely round it; and it is flanked with strong towers at ten foot distance. I stepped over the great western gate and passed very gently, and sideling through the two principal streets, only in my short waistcoat, for fear of damaging the roofs and eaves of the houses with the skirts of my coat. I walked with the utmost circumspection, to avoid treading on any stragglers who might remain in the streets, although the orders were very strict, that all people should keep in their houses, at their own peril. The garret windows and tops of houses were so crowded with spectators, that I thought in all my travels I had not seen a more populous place.

One morning, about a fortnight after I had obtained my liberty, Reldresal, Principal Secretary of Private Affairs, came to my house. He ordered his coach to wait at a distance, and desired I would give him an hour's audience: which I readily consented to on account of his quality and personal merits, as well as of the many good offices he had done me during my solicitations at Court. I offered to lie down, that he might the more conveniently reach my ear; but he chose rather to let me hold him in my hand during our conversation.

He began with compliments on my liberty, said he might pretend to some merit in it; but however, added that if it had not been for the present situation of things at court, perhaps I might not have obtained it so soon. For, said he, "As flourishing a condition as we appear to be in to foreigners, we labour under two mighty evils; a violent faction at home, and the danger of an invasion by a most potent enemy from abroad. As to the first, you are to understand, that for above seventy moons past, there have been two struggling parties in this Empire under the names of *Tramecksan* and *Slamecksan*, from the high and low heels on their shoes, by which they distinguish themselves. It is alleged indeed, that the high heels are most agreeable to our ancient constitution; but however this be, His Majesty hath determined to make use of only low heels in the administration of the government, and all offices in the gift of the Crown. The animosities between these two parties run so high, that they will neither eat nor drink, nor talk with each other. We compute the *Tramecksan*, or High-Heels, to exceed us in number; but the power is wholly on our side. We apprehend His Imperial Highness, the heir to the Crown, to have some tendency towards the High-Heels; at least we can plainly discover one of his heels higher than the other, which gives him a hobble in his gait.

"Now, in the midst of these intense disquiets, we are threatened with an invasion from the island of Blefuscu, which is the other great Empire of the universe, almost as large and powerful as this of His Majesty. For as to what we have heard you affirm, that there are other kingdoms and states in the world, inhibited by human creatures as large as yourself, our philosophers are in much doubt, and would rather conjecture that you dropped from the moon, or one of the stars; because it is certain, that an hundred mortals of your bulk would, in a short time, destroy all the fruits and cattle of His Majesty's dominions. Besides, our histories of six thousand moons make no mention of any other regions, than the two great Empires of Lilliput and Blefuscu; which two mighty powers have, as I was going to tell you, been engaged in a most obstinate war for six and thirty moons past.

"It began upon the following occasion: it is allowed on all hands, that the primitive way of breaking eggs before we eat them, was upon the larger end; but His present Majesty's grandfather, while he was a boy, going to eat an egg, and breaking it according to the ancient practice, happened to cut one of his fingers. Whereupon, the Emperor his father published an edict, commanding all his subjects, upon great penalties, to break the smaller end of their eggs. The people so highly resented this law, that our histories tell us there have been six rebellions raised on that account; wherein one Emperor lost his life, and another his crown. These civil commotions were constantly fomented by the monarchs of Blefuscu; and when they were quelled, the exiles always fled for refuge to that Empire. It is computed that eleven thousand persons have, at several times, suffered death rather than submit to break their eggs at the smaller end. Many hundred large volumes have been published upon this controversy; but the books of the Big-Endians have been long forbidden, and the whole party rendered incapable by law of holding employments. During the course of these troubles, the Emperors of Blefuscu did frequently expostulate by their ambassadors, accusing us of making a schism in religion, by offending against a fundamental doctrine of our great Prophet. This, however, is thought to be a mere strain upon the text, for the words are these: *That all true believers shall break their eggs at the convenient end*: and which is the convenient end, seems, in my humble opinion, to be left to every man's conscience, or at least in the power of the chief magistrate to determine.

"Now the Big-Endian exiles have found so much credit in the Emperor of Blefuscu's court, and so much private assistance and encouragement from their party here at home, that a bloody war hath been carried on between the two Empires for six and thirty moons with various success; during which time we have lost forty capital ships, and a much greater number of smaller vessels, together with thirty thousand of our best seamen and soldiers; and the damage received by the enemy is reckoned to be somewhat greater than ours. However, they have now equipped a numerous fleet and are just preparing to make a descent upon us; and His Imperial Majesty, placing great confidence in your valour and strength, hath commanded me to lay this account of his affairs before you."

I desired the Secretary to present my humble duty to the Emperor and to let him know that I thought it would not become me, a foreigner, to interfere with parties; but I was ready, with the hazard of my life, to defend his person and state against all invaders.

CHAPTER FIVE

GULLIVER PREVENTS AN INVASION

The Empire of Blefuscu is an island situated to the north-north-east side of Lilliput, from whence it is parted only by a channel eight hundred yards wide. I had not yet seen it, and upon this notice of an intended invasion, I avoided appearing on that side of the coast, for fear of being discovered by some of the enemy's ships, who had received no intelligence of me, all intercourse between the two empires having been strictly forbidden during the war, upon pain of death, and an embargo laid by our emperor upon all vessels whatsoever.

I communicated to His Majesty a project I had formed of seizing the enemy's whole fleet; which, as our scouts assured us, lay at anchor in the harbour, ready to sail with the first fair wind. I walked to the north-east coast over against Blefuscu; where, lying down behind a hillock, I took out my small pocket perspective-glass, and viewed the enemy's fleet at anchor, consisting of about fifty men-of-war, and a great number of transports: I then came back to my house, and gave order (for which I had a warrant) for a great quantity of the strongest cable and bars of iron. The cable was about as thick as packthread, and the bars of the length and size of a knitting-needle. I trebled the cable to make it stronger, and for the same reason I twisted three of the iron bars together, bending the extremities into a hook. Having thus fixed fifty hooks to as many cables, I went back to the north-east coast, and putting off my coat, shoes, and stockings, walked into the sea in my leathern jerkin about half an hour before high water. I waded with what haste I could, and swam in the middle about thirty yards till I felt ground. I arrived at the fleet in less than half an hour.

The enemy was so frightened when they saw me, that they leaped out of their ships, and swam to shore. I then took my tackling, and fastening a hook to the hole at the prow of each, I tied all the cords together at the end. While I was thus employed, the enemy discharged several thousand arrows, many of which stuck in my hands and face; and besides the excessive smart, gave me much disturbance in my work. My greatest apprehension was for mine eyes, which I should have infallibly lost, if I had not suddenly thought of an expedient. I kept among other little necessaries, a pair of spectacles in a private pocket, which, as I observed before, had escaped the Emperor's searchers. These I took out and fastened as strongly as I could upon my nose, and thus armed, went on boldly with my work in spite of the enemy's arrows, many of which struck against the glasses of my spectacles, but without any other effect, further than a little to discompose them. I had now fastened all the hooks, and taking the knot in my hand, began to pull; but not a ship would stir, for they were all too fast held by their anchors, so that the boldest part of my enterprise remained. I therefore let go the cord, and leaving the hooks fixed to the ships, I resolutely cut with my knife the cables that fastened the anchors, receiving above two hundred shots in my face and hands; then I took up the knotted end of the cables to which my hooks were tied, and with great ease drew fifty of the enemy's largest men-of-war after me.

The Emperor and his whole Court stood on the shore expecting the issue of this great adventure. They saw the ships move forward in a large half-moon, but could not discern me who was up to my breast in water. When I advanced to the middle of the channel, they were yet more in pain, because I was under water to my neck. The Emperor concluded me to be drowned, and that the enemy's fleet was approaching in a hostile manner: but he was soon eased of his fears, for the channel growing shallower every step I made, I came in a short time within hearing, and holding up the end of the cable by which the fleet was fastened, I cried in a loud voice, *Long live the most puissant Emperor of Lilliput!* This great prince received me at my landing with all possible encomiums, and created me a *Nardac* upon the spot, which is the highest title of honour among them.

His Majesty desired I would take some other opportunity of bringing all the rest of his enemy's ships into his ports. And so unmeasurable is the ambition of princes, that he seemed to think of nothing less than reducing the whole Empire of Blefuscu into a province, and governing it by a Viceroy; of destroying the Big-Endian exiles, and compelling that people to break the smaller end of their eggs, by which he would remain sole monarch of the whole world. But I endeavoured to divert him from this design, by many arguments drawn from the topics of policy as well as justice: and I plainly protested, that I would never be an instrument of bringing a free and brave people into slavery. And when the matter was debated in Council, the wisest part of the Ministry were of my opinion.

This open, bold declaration of mine was so opposite to the schemes and politics of His Imperial Majesty, that he could never forgive me; he mentioned it in a very artful manner at Council, where I was told that some of the wisest appeared, at least by their silence, to be of my opinion; but others, who were my secret enemies, could not forbear some expressions, which by a side-wind reflected on me. Of so little weight are the greatest services to princes, when put into the balance with a refusal to gratify their passions.

About three weeks after this exploit, there arrived a solemn embassy from Blefuscu, with humble offers of a peace. They invited me to that kingdom in their master's name, which our Emperor granted me.

CHAPTER SIX

ESCAPE TO BLEFUSCU

Before I proceed to give an account of my leaving this kingdom, it may be proper to inform the reader of a private intrigue which had been for two months forming against me.

When I was just preparing to pay my attendance on the Emperor of Blefuscu, a considerable person at Court came to my house very privately at night in a closed chair, and without sending his name, desired admittance. The chairmen were dismissed, I put the chair, with his Lordship in it, into my coat-pocket; and giving orders to a trusty servant to say I was indisposed and gone to sleep, I fastened the door of my house, placed the chair on the table, according to my usual custom, and sat down by it. After the common salutations were over, observing his Lordship's countenance full of concern, and enquiring into the reason, he desired I would hear him with patience in a matter that highly concerned my honour and my life.

You are to know, said he, that several Committees of Council have been lately called in the most private manner on your account, and it is but two days since His Majesty came to a full resolution.

You are very sensible that Skyresh Bolgolam hath been your mortal enemy almost ever since your arrival. His hatred is much increased since your great success against Blefuscu, by which his glory as Admiral is obscured. This Lord, in conjunction with Flimnap the High Treasurer, has prepared articles of impeachment against you, for treason, and other capital crimes.

This preface made me so impatient, being conscious of my own merits and innocence, that I was going to interrupt, when he entreated me to be silent, and thus proceeded:

"Out of gratitude for the favours you have done me, I procured information of the whole proceedings. In the several debates upon this impeachment, His Majesty gave many marks of his great lenity, often urging the services you had done him, and endeavouring to extenuate your crimes. The Treasurer and Admiral insisted that you should be put to the most painful and ignominious death, by setting fire on your house at night, and the General was to attend with twenty thousand men armed with poisoned arrows, to shoot you on the face and hands. Some of your servants were to have private orders to strew a poisonous juice on your shirts and sheets, which would soon make you tear your own flesh, and die in the utmost torture. His Majesty resolving, if possible, to spare your life, commanded your friend Reldresal to deliver his opinion.

"Reldresal allowed your crimes to be great, but that still there was room for mercy—the most commendable virtue in a prince, and for which His Majesty was so justly celebrated. He said that if His Majesty, in consideration of your services, and pursuant to his own merciful disposition, would please to spare your life, and only give order to put out both your eyes, justice might in some measure be satisfied, and all the world would applaud the lenity of the Emperor, as well as the fair and generous proceedings of those who have the honour to be his counsellors.

"This proposal was received with the utmost disapprobation by the whole board. His Imperial Majesty, fully determined against capital punishment, was graciously pleased to say, that since the Council thought the loss of your eyes too easy a censure, some other may be inflicted hereafter. And your friend the Secretary, humbly desiring to be heard again, in answer to the great charge His Majesty was at in maintaining you, said that his Excellency might easily provide against this evil by gradually lessening your establishment; and by this, for want of sufficient food, you would grow weak and faint, and lose your appetite, and consequently decay and perish in a few months. Neither would the stench of your carcass be then so dangerous, when it should become more than half diminished, and immediately upon your death, five or six thousand of His Majesty's subjects might, in two or three days, cut your flesh from your bones, take it away by cart-loads, and bury it in distant parts to prevent infection, leaving the skeleton as a monument of admiration to posterity. Thus by the great friendship of the Secretary, the whole affair was compromised.

"In three days your friend the Secretary will be directed to come to your house, and read before you the articles of impeachment; and then to signify the great lenity and favour of His Majesty and Council, whereby you are only condemned to the loss of your eyes, which His Majesty doth not question you will gratefully and humbly submit to; and twenty of His Majesty's surgeons will attend, in order to see the operation well performed, by discharging very sharp-pointed arrows into the balls of your eyes, as you lie on the ground."

His Lordship took his leave and I remained alone, under many doubts and perplexities of mind.

I sometimes thought of standing my trial, for although I could not deny the facts alleged in the several articles, yet I hoped they would admit of some extenuations. But having in my life perused many state trials, which I ever observed to terminate as judges thought fit to direct, I dare not rely on so dangerous a decision, in so critical a juncture, and against such powerful enemies. Once I was strongly bent upon resistance, for while I had liberty, the whole strength of the Empire could hardly subdue me, and I might easily with stones pelt the metropolis to pieces; but I soon rejected that project with horror, by remembering the oath I had made to the Emperor, the favours I received from him and the high title of *Nardac* he conferred upon me.

At last I fixed upon a resolution, for which it is probable I may incur some censure, and not unjustly. Having His Imperial Majesty's licence to pay my attendance upon the Emperor of Blefuscu, I took this opportunity, before the three days were elapsed, to send a letter to my friend the Secretary, signifying my resolution of setting out that morning for Blefuscu, pursuant to the leave I had got; and without waiting for an answer, I went to that side of the island where our fleet lay. I seized a large man-of-war, tied a cable to the prow, and lifting up the anchors, I stripped myself, put my clothes into the vessel, and drawing it after me between wading and swimming, arrived at the royal port of Blefuscu, where the people had long expected me; they lent me two guides to direct me to the capital city, which is of the same name. I held them in my hands till I came within two hundred yards of the gate, and desired them to signify my arrival to one of the Secretaries, and let him know, I there waited His Majesty's commands. I had an answer in about an hour, that His Majesty, attended by the family, and great officers of the court, was coming out to receive me. I advanced a hundred yards. The Emperor and his train alighted from their horses, the Empress and ladies from their coaches, and I did not perceive they were in any fright or concern. I lay on the ground to kiss His Majesty's and the Empress' hand. I told His Majesty that I was come according to my promise, and with the licence of the Emperor my master, to have the honour of seeing so mighty a monarch and to offer him any service in my power, consistent with my duty to my own Prince; not mentioning a word of my disgrace, because I had hitherto no regular information of it, and might suppose myself wholly ignorant of any such design.

CHAPTER SEVEN

GULLIVER RETURNS HOME

Three days after my arrival, walking out of curiosity to the north-east coast of the island, I observed, about half a league off in the sea, something that looked like a boat overturned. I found the object to approach nearer by force of the tide, and then plainly saw it to be a real boat. I returned immediately towards the city, and desired His Imperial Majesty to lend me twenty of the tallest vessels he had left after the loss of his fleet, and three thousand seamen under the command of his Vice-Admiral. The seamen were all provided with cordage, which I had beforehand twisted to a sufficient strength. I took out my other cables, which were stowed in one of the ships, and fastening them first to the boat, and then to nine of the vessels which attended me; the wind being favourable, the seamen towed, and I shoved till we arrived within forty yards of the shore; and waiting till the tide was out, I got dry to the boat, and by the assistance of two thousand men, with ropes and engines, I made a shift to turn it on its bottom and found it was but little damaged.

I told the Emperor that my good fortune had thrown this boat in my way to carry me to some place from whence I might return into my native country, and begged His Majesty's orders for getting materials to fit it up, together with his licence to depart; which, after some kind expostulations, he was pleased to grant.

In about a month, when all was prepared, I sent to receive His Majesty's commands and to take my leave. The Emperor and the royal family came out of the palace; I lay down on my face to kiss his hand, which he very graciously gave me; so did the Empress, and young princes of the blood.

I stored the boat with the carcasses of an hundred oxen and three hundred sheep, with bread and drink proportionable, and as much meat ready dressed as four hundred cooks could provide. I took with me six cows and two bulls alive, with as many ewes and rams, intending to carry them into my own country, and propagate the breed. And to feed them on board, I had a good bundle of hay and a bag of corn. I would gladly have taken a dozen of the natives, but this was a thing the Emperor would by no means permit; and besides a diligent search into my pockets, His Majesty engaged my honour not to carry away any of his subjects, although with their own consent and desire.

Having thus prepared all things as well as I was able, I set sail on the twenty-fourth day of September, 1701, at six in the morning; and when I had gone about four leagues I descried a small island about half a league to the north-west. I advanced forward, and cast anchor on the lee-side of the island, which seemed to be uninhabited. I then took some refreshment, and went to my rest. The next morning I steered the same course that I had done the day before, wherein I was directed by my pocket-compass. I discovered nothing all that day; but upon the next, about three in the afternoon, I descried a sail steering to the south-east. I hailed her, and in half an hour she spied me, then hung out her antient, and discharged a gun. It is not easy to express the joy I was in upon the unexpected hope of once more seeing my beloved country, and the dear pledges I had left in it. The ship slackened her sails, and I came up with her between five and six in the evening, 26th September; but my heart leapt within me to see her English colours. I put my cows and sheep into my coat-pockets, and got on board with all my little cargo of provisions. The vessel was an English merchantman returning from Japan; the captain, Mr John Biddel of Deptford, a very civil man, and an excellent sailor. There were about fifty men in the ship; and here I met an old comrade of mine, one Peter Williams, who gave me a good character to the captain. This gentleman treated me with kindness, and desired I would let him know what place I came from last, and whither I was bound; which I did in few words, but he thought I was raving, and that the dangers underwent had disturbed my head; whereupon I took my cattle and sheep out of my pocket, which, after great astonishment, clearly convinced him of my veracity.

We arrived in the Downs on the 13th of April, 1702. I had only one misfortune, that the rats on board carried away one of my sheep; I found her bones in a hole, picked clean from the flesh. The rest of my cattle I got safe on shore, and set them grazing in a bowling-green at Greenwich, where the fineness of the grass made them feed very heartily, though I had always feared the contrary: neither could I possibly have preserved them in so long a voyage, if the captain had not allowed me some of his best biscuit, which, rubbed to powder and mingled with water, was their constant food. The short time I continued in England, I made a considerable profit by showing my cattle to many persons of quality, and others, and before I began my second voyage, I sold them for six hundred pounds. Since my last return, I find the breed is considerably increased, especially the sheep; which I hope will prove much to the advantage of the woollen manufacture, by the fineness of the fleeces.

PART II: A VOYAGE TO BROBDINGNAG

CHAPTER ONE: GULLIVER IS CARRIED TO A FARMER'S HOUSE

Having been condemned by nature and fortune to an active and restless life, in two months after my return I again left my native country, and took shipping in the Downs on the 20th day of June, 1702, in the *Adventure*, Capt. John Nicholas, a Cornish man, commander, bound for Surat. We had a very prosperous gale till we arrived at the Cape of Good Hope, where we landed for fresh water, but discovering a leak, we unshipped our goods and wintered there; for the captain falling sick of an ague, we could not leave the Cape till the end of March. We then set sail; and had a good voyage till we passed the Straits of Madagascar.

On the 16th day of June, 1703, a boy on the top-mast discovered land. On the 17th we came in full view of a great island or continent. We cast anchor and our captain sent a dozen of his men well armed in the long-boat, with vessels for water if any could be found. I desired his leave to go with them, that I might see the country, and make what discoveries I could. When we came to land we saw no river or spring, nor any sign of inhabitants. Our men therefore wandered on the shore to find out some fresh water near the sea, and I walked alone about a mile on the other side, where I observed the country all barren and rocky. I now began to be weary, and seeing nothing to entertain my curiosity, I returned gently down towards the creek; and the sea being full in my view, I saw our men already got into the boat, and rowing for life to the ship. I was going to halloo after them, although it had been to little purpose, when I observed a huge creature walking after them in the sea, as fast as he could. He waded not much deeper than his knees, and took prodigious strides: but our men had the start of him by half a league, and the sea thereabouts being full of sharp-pointed rocks, the monster was not able to overtake the boat. I did not dare to stay to see the issue of that adventure, but ran as fast as I could the way I first went; and then climbed up a steep hill, which gave me some prospect of the country. I found it fully cultivated; but that which first surprised me was the length of the grass, which in those grounds that seemed to be kept for hay, was above twenty foot high.

I walked on for some time, but could see little on either side, it being now near harvest, and the corn rising at least forty foot. I was an hour walking to the end of this field, which was fenced in with a hedge at least one hundred and twenty foot high, and the trees so lofty that I could make no computation of their altitude. There was a stile to pass from this field into the next. It was impossible for me to climb this stile, because every step was six foot high and the upper stone above twenty. I was endeavouring to find some gap in the hedge, when I discovered one of the inhabitants in the next field advancing towards the stile, of the same size with him whom I saw in the sea pursuing our boat. He appeared as tall as an ordinary spire-steeple, and took about ten yards at every stride, as near as I could guess. I was struck with the utmost fear and astonishment, and ran to hide myself in the corn, from whence I saw him at the top of the stile, looking back into the next field on the right hand, and heard him call in a voice many degrees louder than a speaking-trumpet; but the noise was so high in the air, that at first I certainly thought it was thunder. Whereupon, seven monsters like himself came towards him with reaping-hooks in their hands, each hook about the largeness of six scythes. These people were not so well clad as the first, whose servants or labourers they seemed to be:

for upon some words he spoke, they went to reap the corn in the field where I lay. I kept from them at as great a distance as I could, but was forced to move with extreme difficulty, for the stalks of the corn were sometimes not above a foot distant, so that I could hardly squeeze my body betwixt them. However, I made a shift to go forward till I came to a part of the field where the corn had been laid by the rain and wind. Here it was impossible for me to advance a step: for the stalks were so interwoven that I could not creep through, and the beards of the fallen ears so strong and pointed that they pierced through my clothes into my flesh. At the same time I heard the reapers not above an hundred yards behind me. Being quite dispirited with toil, and wholly overcome by grief and despair, I lay down between two ridges, and heartily wished I might there end my days. I bemoaned my desolate widow and fatherless children. I lamented my own folly and wilfulness in attempting a second voyage against the advice of all my friends and relations.

Scared and confounded as I was, I could not forbear going on with these reflections, when one of the reapers approaching within ten yards of the ridge where I lay, made me apprehend that with the next step I should be squashed to death under his foot, or cut in two with his reaping-hook. And therefore when he was again about to move, I screamed as loud as fear could make me. Whereupon the huge creature trod short, and looking round about under him for some time, at last espied me as I lay on the ground. He considered a while with the caution of one who endeavours to lay hold on a small dangerous animal in such a manner that it shall not be able either to scratch or to bite him, as I myself have sometimes done with a weasel in England. At length he ventured to take me up behind by the middle between his forefinger and thumb, and brought me within three yards of his eyes, that he might behold my shape more perfectly. I guessed his meaning, and my good fortune gave me so much presence of mind, that I resolved not to struggle in the least as he held me in the air above sixty foot from the ground, although he grievously pinched my sides, for fear I should slip through his fingers. All I ventured was to raise mine eyes towards the sun, and place my hands together in a supplicating posture, and to speak some words in an humble melancholy tone, suitable to the condition I then was in. For I apprehended every moment that he would dash me against the ground, as we usually do any little hateful animal which we have a mind to destroy. But my good star would have it, that he appeared pleased with my voice and gestures, and began to look upon me as a curiosity, much wondering to hear me pronounce articulate words, although he could not understand them. In the meantime I was not able to forbear groaning and shedding tears, and turning my head towards my sides; letting him know, as well as I could, how cruelly I was hurt by the pressure of his thumb and finger. He seemed to apprehend my meaning, for lifting up the lappet of his coat, he put me gently into it, and immediately ran along with me to his master, who was a substantial farmer, and the same person I had first seen in the field.

The farmer spoke to me, but the sound of his voice pierced my ears like that of a watermill, yet his words were articulate enough. I answered as loud as I could in several languages, and he often laid his ear within two yards of me, but all in vain, for we were wholly unintelligible to each other. He then sent his servants to their work, and taking his handkerchief out of his pocket, he doubled and spread it on his left hand, which he placed flat on the ground with the palm upwards, making me a sign to step into it, as I could easily do, for it was not above a foot in thickness. I thought it my part to obey; and for fear of falling, laid myself at full length upon the handkerchief, with the remainder of which he lapped me up to the head for further security, and in this manner carried me home to his house. There he called his wife and showed me to her; but she screamed and ran back as women in England do at the sight of a toad or a spider. However, when she had a while seen my behaviour, and how well I observed the signs her husband made, she was soon reconciled, and by degrees grew extremely tender of me.

It was about twelve at noon, and a servant brought in dinner. It was only one substantial dish of meat in a dish of about four and twenty foot diameter. The company were the farmer and his wife, three children, and an old grandmother. When they were sat down, the farmer placed me at some distance from him on the table, which was thirty foot high from the floor. I was in a terrible fright, and kept as far as I could from the edge for fear of falling. The wife minced a bit of meat, then crumbled some bread on a trencher, and placed it before me. I made her a low bow, took out my knife and fork, and fell to eat, which gave them exceeding delight. The mistress sent her maid for a small dram-cup, which held about two gallons, and filled it with drink; I took up the vessel with much difficulty in both hands and in a most respectful manner drank to her ladyship's health, expressing the words as loud as I could in English, which made the company laugh so heartily, that I was almost deafened with the noise. Then the master made me a sign to come to his trencher side; but as I walked on the table, being in great surprise all the time, I happened to stumble against a crust, and fell on my face, but received no hurt.

When dinner was almost done, the nurse came in with a child of a year old in her arms, who immediately spied me, and began a squall that you might have heard from London Bridge to Chelsea, after the usual oratory of infants, to get me for a plaything. The mother out of pure indulgence took me up, and put me towards the child, who presently seized me by the middle, and got my head in his mouth, where I roared so loud that the urchin was frightened, and let me drop, and I should infallibly have broken my neck if the mother had not held her apron under me. The nurse, to quiet her babe, made use of a rattle: but all in vain, so that she was forced to apply the last remedy by giving it suck. I must confess no object ever disgusted me so much as the sight of her monstrous breast, which I cannot tell what to compare with, so as to give the curious reader an idea of its bulk, shape and colour. It stood prominent six foot, and could not be less than sixteen in circumference. The nipple was about half the bigness of my head, and the hue both of that and the dug so varified with spots, pimples and freckles, that nothing could appear more nauseous: for I had a near sight of her, she sitting down the more conveniently to give suck, and I standing on the table. This made me reflect upon the fair skins of our English ladies, who appear so beautiful to us, only because they are of our own size, and their defects not to be seen but through a magnifying glass, where we find by experiment that the smoothest and whitest skins look rough and coarse, and ill-coloured.

When dinner was done, my master went out to his labourers and as I could discover by his voice and gesture, gave his wife a strict charge to take care of me. I was very much tired and disposed to sleep, which my mistress perceiving, she put me on her own bed, and covered me with a clear white handkerchief but larger and coarser than the main sail of a man-of-war.

CHAPTER TWO

GULLIVER EXHIBITED IN MARKET-PLACES

My mistress had a daughter nine years old, a child of towardly parts for her age, very dexterous at her needle, and skilful in dressing her baby. Her mother and she contrived to fit up the baby's cradle for me against night: the cradle was put into a small drawer of a cabinet, and the drawer placed upon a hanging shelf for fear of the rats. This was my bed all the time I stayed with those people, though made more convenient by degrees, as I began to learn their language, and make my wants known. This young girl was so handy, that after I had once or twice pulled off my clothes before her, she was able to dress and undress me, although I never gave her that trouble when she would let me do either myself. She made me seven shirts, and some other linen, of as fine cloth as could be got, which indeed was coarser than sackcloth; and these she constantly washed for me with her own hands. She was likewise my school-mistress to teach me the language. When I pointed to anything, she told me the name of it in her own tongue, so that in a few days I was able to call for whatever I had a mind to. She was very good-natured, and not above forty foot high, being little for her age. To her I chiefly owe my preservation in that country: we never parted while I was there; I called her my *glumdalclitch*, or 'little nurse': and I should be guilty of great ingratitude if I omitted this honourable mention of the care and affection towards me, which I heartily wish it lay in my power to requite as she deserves, instead of being the innocent but unhappy instrument of her disgrace, as I have too much reason to fear.

It now began to be known and talked of in the neighbourhood, that my master had found a strange animal in the fields, about the bigness of a *splacnuck*, but exactly shaped in every part like a human creature, which it likewise imitated in all its actions; seemed to speak in a little language of its own, had already learned several words of theirs, went erect upon two legs, was tame and gentle, would come when it was called, do whatever it was bid, had the finest limbs in the world, and a complexion fairer than a nobleman's daughter of three years age.

Another farmer who lived hard by, and was a particular friend of my master, came on a visit on purpose to enquire into the truth of this story. I was immediately produced, and placed upon a table, where I walked as I was commanded, drew my hanger, put it up again, made my reverence to my master's guest, asked him in his own language how he did, and told him he was welcome, just as my little nurse had instructed me. This man, who was old and dim-sighted, put on his spectacles to behold me better, at which I could not forbear laughing very heartily, for his eyes appeared like the full moon shining into a chamber at two windows. Our people, who discovered the cause of my mirth, bore me company in laughing, at which the old fellow was fool enough to be angry and out of countenance. He had the character of a great miser, and to my misfortune he well deserved it by the cursed advice he gave my master to show me as a sight upon a market-day in the next town, which was half an hour's riding, about two and twenty miles from our house. I guessed there was some mischief contriving, when I observed my master and his friend whispering long together, sometimes pointing at me; and my fears made me fancy that I overheard and understood some of their words.

The next morning Glumdalclitch, my little nurse, told me the whole matter, which she had cunningly picked out from her mother. The poor girl laid me on her bosom, and fell a-weeping with shame and grief. She apprehended some mischief would happen to me from rude vulgar folks, who might squeeze me to death or break one of my limbs by taking me in their hands. She had also observed how modest I was in my nature, how nicely I regarded my honour, and what an indignity I should conceive it to be exposed for money as a public spectacle to the meanest of the people.

My master, pursuant to the advice of his friend, carried me in a box the next market-day to the neighbouring town, and took along with him his little daughter, my nurse, upon a pillion behind him. The box was closed on every side, with a little door for me to go in and out, and a few gimlet-holes to let in air. The girl had been so careful to put the quilt of her baby's bed into it, for me to lie down on. However, I was terribly shaken and discomposed in this journey, though it was but half an hour. For the horse went about forty foot at every step, and trotted so high, that the agitation was equal to the rising and falling of a ship in a great storm, but much more frequent. My master alighted at an inn which he used to frequent, and after consulting a while with the innkeeper and making some necessary preparations, he hired the Crier to give notice through the town, of a strange creature to be seen at the Sign of the Green Eagle.

I was placed upon a table in the largest room of the inn, which might be near three hundred foot square. My little nurse stood on a low stool close to the table, to take care of me and direct what I should do. My master, to avoid a crowd, would suffer only thirty people at a time to see me. I walked about on the table as the girl commanded; she asked me questions as far as she knew my understanding of the language reached, and I answered them as loud as I could. I turned about several times to the company, paid my humble respects, said they were welcome, and used some other speeches I had been taught. I took up a thimble filled with liquor, which Glumdalclitch had given me for a cup, and drank to their health. I drew out my hanger and flourished with it after the manner of fencers in England. My nurse gave me part of a straw, which I exercised as a pike, having learned the art in my youth. I was that day shown to twelve sets of company, and as often forced to go over again with the same fopperies, till I was half dead with weariness and vexation. For those who had seen me made such wonderful reports, that the people were ready to break down the doors to come in. My master for his own interest would not suffer anyone to touch me except my nurse; and, to prevent danger, benches were set round the table at such a distance as put me out of everybody's reach. However, an unlucky school-boy aimed a hazel nut directly at my head, which very narrowly missed me; otherwise, it came with so much violence that it would have infallibly knocked out my brains—but I had the satisfaction to see the young rogue well beaten, and turned out of the room.

My master, finding how profitable I was like to be, resolved to carry me to the most considerable cities of the kingdom. Having therefore provided himself with all things necessary for a long journey, and settled his affairs at home, he took leave of his wife. Upon the 17th of August, 1703, about two months after my arrival, we set out for the metropolis situated near the middle of that Empire, and about three thousand miles distance from our house. My master made his daughter Glumdalclitch ride behind him. She carried me on her lap in a box tied about her waist. The girl had lined it on all sides with the softest cloth she could get, well quilted underneath, furnished it with her baby's bed, provided me with linen and other necessaries, and made everything as convenient as she could. We had no other company but a boy of the house, who rode after us with the luggage.

On the 26th day of October, we arrived at the metropolis, called in their language *Lorbrulgrud*, or *Pride of the Universe*. My master took a lodging in the principal street of the city, not far from the royal palace, and put out bills in the usual form, containing an exact description of my person and parts. He hired a large room between three and four hundred foot wide. He provided a table sixty foot in diameter, upon which I was to act my part, and palisadoed it round three foot from the edge, and as many high, to prevent my falling over. I was shown ten times a day to the wonder and satisfaction of all people. I could now speak the language tolerably well, and perfectly understood every word that was spoken to me. Besides I had learnt their alphabet, and could make a shift to explain a sentence here and there, for Glumdalclitch had been my instructor while we were at home, and at leisure hours during our journey.

CHAPTER THREE

GULLIVER IN THE ROYAL COURT

The frequent labours I underwent every day, made in a few weeks a very considerable change in my health. The more my master got by me, the more unsatiable he grew. I had quite lost my stomach, and was almost reduced to a skeleton. The farmer observed it, and concluding I soon must die, resolved to make as good a hand of me as he could. While he was thus reasoning and resolving with himself, a Gentleman Usher came from Court, commanding my master to bring me immediately thither for the diversion of the Queen and her ladies. Some of the latter had already been to see me, and reported strange things of my beauty, behaviour, and good sense. Her Majesty and those who attended her were beyond measure delighted with my demeanour. I fell on my knees, and begged the honour of kissing her imperial foot; but this gracious Princess held out her little finger towards me (after I was set on a table) which I embraced in both my arms, and put the tip of it, with the utmost respect, to my lips. She made me some general questions about my country and my travels, which I answered as distinctly and in as few words as I could. She asked whether I would be content to live at Court. I bowed down to the board of the table, and humbly answered that I was my master's slave, but if I were at my own disposal, I should be proud to devote my life to Her Majesty's service. She then asked my master whether he were willing to sell me at a good price. He, who apprehended I could not live a month, was ready enough to part with me, and demanded a thousand pieces of gold, which were ordered for him on the spot. I then said to the Queen, since I was now Her Majesty's most humble creature and vassal, I must beg the favour, that Glumdalclitch, who had always tended me with so much care and kindness and understood to do it so well, might be admitted into her service, and continue to be my nurse and instructor. Her Majesty agreed to my petition and easily got the farmer's consent, who was glad enough to have his daughter preferred at Court, and the poor girl herself was not able to hide her joy. My late master withdrew, bidding me farewell, and saying he had left me in a good service, to which I replied not a word.

The Queen, giving great allowance for my defectiveness in speaking, was however surprised at so much wit and good sense in so diminutive an animal. She took me in her own hand, and carried me to the King. She commanded me to give His Majesty an account of myself, which I did in very few words; and Glumdalclitch confirmed all that had passed since my arrival at her father's house.

I applied myself to the King, and assured His Majesty that I came from a country which abounded with several millions of both sexes, and of my own stature; where the animals, trees, and houses were all in proportion, and where by consequence I might be as able to defend myself, and to find sustenance, as any of His Majesty's subjects could do here. The King sent for the farmer, who by good fortune was not yet gone out of town. Having therefore first examined him privately, and then confronted him with me and the young girl, His Majesty began to think that what we told him might possibly be true. He desired the Queen to order that particular care should be taken of me, and was of the opinion that Glumdalclitch should still continue in her office of tending me, because he observed we had a great affection for each other. A convenient apartment was provided for her at Court. She had a sort of governess appointed to take care of her education, a maid to dress her, and two other servants for menial offices; but the care of me was wholly appropriated to herself. The Queen commanded her own cabinet-maker to contrive a box that might serve me for a bed-chamber, after the model that Glumdalclitch and I should agree upon. This man was a most ingenious artist, and according to my directions, in three weeks finished for me a wooden chamber of sixteen foot square, and twelve high, with sash-windows, a door, and two closets, like a London bed-chamber. I made a shift to keep the key of the chamber in a pocket of my own, fearing Glumdalclitch might lose it. The Queen likewise ordered the thinnest silks that could be gotten, to make me clothes, not much thicker than an English blanket, very cumbersome till I was accustomed to them.

The Queen became so fond of my company that she could not dine without me. I had a table placed upon the same at which Her Majesty ate, just at her left elbow, and a chair to sit on. Glumdalclitch stood upon a stool on the floor, near my table, to assist and take care of me.

The King took a pleasure in conversing with me, enquiring into the manners, religion, laws, government, and learning of Europe, wherein I gave him the best account I was able. His apprehension was so clear, and his judgement so exact, that he made very wide reflections and observations upon all I said. But, I confess that after I had been a little too copious in talking of my own beloved country—of our trade, and wars by sea and land, of our schisms in religion, and parties in the state—the prejudices of his education prevailed so far, that he could not forbear taking me up in his right hand, and stroking me gently with the other, after an hearty fit of laughing, asked me whether I were a Whig or a Tory. Then turning to his first Minister, he observed how contemptible a thing was human grandeur, which could be mimicked by such diminutive insects as I. And yet, said he, I dare engage, these creatures have their titles and distinctions of honour; they contrive little nests and burrows that they call houses and cities; they make a figure in dress and equipage; they love, they fight, they dispute, they cheat, they betray. And thus he continued on, while my colour came and went several times with indignation, to hear our noble country, the Mistress of Arts and Arms, the Scourge of France, the Arbitress of Europe, the Seat of Virtue, Piety, Honour and Truth, the Pride and Envy of the World, so contemptuously treated.

Nothing angered and mortified me so much as the Queen's dwarf, who, being of the lowest stature that was ever in that country, became so insolent at seeing a creature so much beneath him that he would always affect to swagger and look big as he passed by me in the Queen's antechamber, while I was standing on some table talking with the Lords or Ladies of the Court. One day at dinner, this malicious little cub was so nettled with something I had said to him, that, raising himself upon the frame of Her Majesty's chair, he took me up by the middle, as I was sitting down, not thinking any harm, and let me drop into a large silver bowl of cream, and then ran away as fast as he could. I fell over head and ears, and if I had not been a good swimmer, it might have gone very hard with me, for Glumdalclitch in that instant happened to be at the other end of the room, and the Queen was in such a fright that she wanted presence of mind to assist me. But my little nurse ran to my relief, and took me out, after I had swallowed above a quart of cream. I was put to bed; however I received no other damage than the loss of a suit of clothes, which was utterly spoiled. The dwarf was soundly whipped, and as a further punishment, forced to drink up the bowl of cream, into which he had thrown me.

CHAPTER FOUR

LORBRULGRUD THE METROPOLIS

Lorbrulgrud stands upon almost two equal parts on each side of the river that passes through. The King's palace is no regular edifice, but an heap of buildings about seven miles around: the chief rooms are generally two hundred and forty foot high, and broad and long in proportion. A coach was allowed to Glumdalclitch and me, wherein her governess frequently took her out to see the town, or go among the shops. And I was always of the party, carried in my box; although the girl at my own desire would often take me out, and hold me in her hand, that I might more conveniently view the houses and the people as we passed along the streets. One day, the governess ordered our coachman to stop at several shops, where the beggars, watching their opportunity, crowded to the sides of the coach, and gave me the most horrible spectacles that ever an European eye beheld. There was a woman with a cancer in her breast, swelled to a monstrous size, full of holes, in two or three of which I could have easily crept.

Besides the large box in which I was usually carried, the Queen ordered a smaller one to be made for me, of about twelve foot square and ten high, for the convenience of travelling, because the other was somewhat too large for Glumdalclitch's lap, and cumbersome in the coach. It was made by the same artist, whom I directed in the whole contrivance. In journeys, when I was weary of the coach, a servant on horseback would buckle my box, and place it on a cushion before him; and there I had a full prospect of the country on three sides from my three windows.

I was very desirous to see the chief temple, and particularly the tower belonging to it, which is reckoned the highest in the kingdom. Accordingly one day, my nurse carried me thither, but I may truly say I came back disappointed, for the height is not above three thousand foot. But it must be allowed that whatever this famous tower wants in height is amply made up in beauty and strength.

CHAPTER FIVE

SEVERAL ADVENTURES THAT HAPPENED TO GULLIVER

I should have lived happily enough in that country, if my littleness had not exposed me to several ridiculous and troublesome accidents. Glumdalclitch often carried me into the gardens of the Court in my smaller box, and would sometimes take me out of it and hold me in her hand, or set me down to walk. I remember, before the dwarf left the Queen, he followed us one day into those gardens, and my nurse having set me down near some dwarf apple-trees, I must needs show my wit by a silly allusion between him and the trees. Whereupon the malicious rogue, watching his opportunity when I was walking under one of them, shook it directly over my head, by which a dozen apples came tumbling about my ears; one of them hit me on the back as I chanced to stoop, and knocked me down flat on my face, but I received no other hurt, and the dwarf was pardoned at my desire, because I had given the provocation.

But, a more dangerous accident happened to me in the same garden, when my little nurse, believing she had put me in a secure place, which I often entreated her to do, that I might enjoy my own thoughts, and having left my box at home to avoid the trouble of carrying it, went to another part of the gardens with her governess and some ladies of her acquaintance. While she was absent and out of hearing, a small white spaniel belonging to one of the chief gardeners, having got by accident into the garden, happened to range near the place where I lay. The dog, following the scent, came directly up, and taking me in his mouth, ran straight to his master, wagging his tail, and set me gently on the ground. By good fortune he had been so well taught, that I was carried between his teeth without the least hurt, or even tearing my clothes. But, the poor gardener who knew me well and had a great kindness for me, was in a terrible fright. He gently took me up in both his hands, and asked me how I did; but I was so amazed and out of breath, that I could not speak a word. In a few minutes I came to myself, and he carried me safe to my little nurse, who by this time had returned to the place where she left me, and was in cruel agonies when I did not appear, nor answer when she called: she severely reprimanded the gardener on account of his dog. But, the thing was hushed up, and never known at court; for the girl was afraid of the Queen's anger, and truly as to myself, I thought it would not be for my reputation that such a story should go about.

The Queen, who often used to hear me talk of my sea voyages, and took all occasions to divert me when I was melancholy, asked me whether I understood how to handle a sail or an oar, and whether a little exercise of rowing might not be convenient for my health. I answered that I understood both very well: for although my proper employment had been to be surgeon or doctor to the ship, yet often, upon a pinch, I was forced to work like a common mariner. The Queen ordered the joiner to make a wooden trough of three hundred foot long, fifty broad, and eight deep; which being well pitched to prevent leaking, was placed on the floor along the wall, in an outer room of the palace. It had a cock stale, and two servants could easily fill it in half an hour. Here I often used to row my own diversion, as well as that of the Queen and her ladies, who thought themselves agreeably entertained with my skill and agility. Sometimes I would put up my sail, and then my business was only to steer, while the ladies gave me a gale with their fans; and when they were weary, some of the pages would blow my sail forward with their breath, while I showed my art of steering starboard or larboard as I pleased. When I had done, Glumdalclitch always carried back my boat into her closet, and hung it on a nail to dry.

In this exercise, I once met with an accident which had like to have cost me my life. For, one of the pages having put my boat into the trough, the governess who attended Glumdalclitch, very officiously lifted me up to place me in the boat, but I happened to slip through her fingers, and should have infallibly fallen down forty foot upon the floor, if by the luckiest chance in the world, I had not been stopped by a corking-pin that stuck in the good gentlewoman's stomacher. The head of the pin passed between my shirt and the waistband of my breeches, and thus I was held by the middle in the air, till Glumdalclitch ran to my relief.

But, the greatest danger I ever underwent in that kingdom was from a monkey. Glumdalclitch had locked me up in her closet, while she went somewhere upon business or a visit. The weather being very warm, the closet window was left open, as well as the windows and the door of my bigger box, in which I usually lived, because of its largeness and conveniency. As I sat quietly meditating at my table, I heard something bounce in at the closet window, and skip about from one side to the other; whereat, although I was much alarmed, I ventured to look out, but not stirring from my seat—and then I saw this frolicsome animal, frisking and leaping up and down, till at last he came to my box, which he seemed to view with great pleasure and curiosity, peeping in at the door and every window. I retreated to the farther corner of my room, or box, but the monkey, looking in at every side, put me into such a fright, that I wanted presence of mind to conceal myself under the bed, as I might easily have done. After some time spent in peeping, grinning, and chattering, he at last espied me; and reaching one of his paws in at the door, as a cat does when she plays with a mouse, although I often shifted place to avoid him, he at length seized the lappet of my coat and dragged me out. He took me up in his tight forefoot, and held me as a nurse doth a child she is going to suckle, just as I have seen the same sort of creature do with a kitten in Europe; and when I offered to struggle, he squeezed me so hard, that I thought it more prudent to submit. I have good reason to believe that he took me for a young one of his own species, by his often stroking my face very gently with his other paw.

In these diversions he was interrupted by a noise at the closet door, as if somebody were opening it; whereupon he suddenly leaped up to the window at which he had come in, and thence upon the leads and gutters, walking upon three legs, and holding me in the fourth, till he clambered up to a roof that was next to ours. I heard Glumdalclitch give a shriek at the moment he was carrying me out. The poor girl was almost distracted: that quarter of the palace was all in an uproar; the servants ran for ladders; the monkey was seen by hundreds in the Court, sitting upon the ridge of a building, holding me like a baby in one of his fore-paws, and feeding me with the other, by cramming into my mouth some victuals he had squeezed out of the bag on one side of his chaps, and patting me when I would not eat—whereat many of the rabble below could not forbear laughing; neither do I think they justly ought to be blamed, for without question the sight was ridiculous enough to everybody but myself. Some of the people threw up stones, hoping to drive the monkey down; but this was strictly forbidden, or else very probably my brains would have been dashed out.

The ladders were now applied and mounted by several men, which the monkey observing and finding himself almost encompassed, not being able to make speed enough with his three legs, let me drop on a ridge tile, and made his escape. Here I sat for some time, five hundred yards from the ground, expecting every moment to be blown down by the wind, or to fall by my own giddiness, and come tumbling over and over from the ridge to the eaves. But an honest lad, one of my nurse's footmen, climbed up, and putting me into his breeches' pocket, brought me down safe.

I was almost choked with the filthy stuff the monkey had crammed down my throat; but, my dear little nurse picked it out of my mouth with a small needle and then I fell a-vomiting, which gave me great relief. Yet I was so weak and bruised in the sides with the squeezes given me by this odious animal, that I was forced to keep my bed a fortnight. The King, Queen and all the Court sent every day to enquire after my health, and Her Majesty made me several visits during my sickness. The monkey was killed, and an order made that no such animal should be kept about the palace.

CHAPTER SIX

HIS MAJESTY'S VIEWS ON EUROPE

The King—who, as I before observed, was a Prince of excellent understanding—would frequently order that I should be brought in my box, and set upon the table in his closet. He would then command me to bring one of my chairs out of the box, and sit down within three yards distance upon the top of the cabinet, which brought me almost to a level with his face. In this manner I had several conversations with him. I one day took the freedom to tell His Majesty, that the contempt he discovered towards Europe and the rest of the world, did not seen answerable to those excellent qualities of mind, that he was master of. The King heard me with attention, and began to conceive a much better opinion of me than he had ever before. He desired I would give him as exact an account of the government of England as I possibly could, because he should be glad to hear of anything that might deserve imitation.

I began my discourse by informing His Majesty that our dominions consisted of two islands, which composed three mighty kingdoms under one sovereign, besides our plantations in America. I dwelt long upon the fertility of our soil, and the temperature of our climate. I then spoke at large upon the constitution of an English Parliament, partly made up of an illustrious body called the House of Peers, persons of the noblest blood, and of the most ancient and ample patrimonies. I described that extraordinary care was always taken of their education in arts and arms, to qualify them for being counsellors born to the King and Kingdom, to have a share in the legislature, to be members of the highest court of judicature from whence there could be no appeal; and to be champions always ready for the defence of their prince and country by their valour, conduct and fidelity. That these were the ornament and bulwark of the kingdom, worthy followers of their most renowned ancestors, whose honour had been the reward of their virtue, from which their posterity were never once know to degenerate. To these were joined several holy persons, as part of that assembly, under the title of Bishops whose peculiar business it is, to take care of religion, and of those who instruct the people therein. These were searched and sought out through the whole nation, by the Prince and his wisest counsellors, among such of the priesthood as were most deservedly distinguished by the sanctity of their lives, and the depth of their erudition; who were indeed the spiritual fathers of the clergy and the people.

That the other part of Parliament consisted of an assembly called the House of Commons, who were all principal gentlemen, *freely* picked and culled out by the people themselves, for their great abilities, and love of their country, to represent the wisdom of the whole nation. And these two bodies make up the most august assembly in Europe, to whom in conjunction with the Prince, the whole legislature is committed.

I then descended to the Courts of Justice, over which the Judges, those venerable sages and interpreters of the law, presided, for determining the disputed rights and the properties of men, as well as for the punishment of vice, and protection of innocence. I mentioned the prudent management of our Treasury, the valour and achievements of our forces by sea and land. I computed the number of our people, by reckoning how many millions there might be of each religious sect, or political party among us. I did not omit even our sports and pastimes, or any other particular which I thought might redound to the honour of my country. And, I finished all with a brief historical account of affairs and events in England for about a hundred years past.

When I had put an end to these long discourses, His Majesty proposed many doubts, queries, and objections, upon every article. He asked what methods were used to cultivate the minds and bodies of our young nobility, and in what kind of business they commonly spent the first and teachable part of their lives. What course was taken to supply that assembly when any noble family became extinct. What qualifications were necessary in those who are to be created new Lords: whether the humour of the Prince, a sum of money to a court lady, or a Prime Minister, or a design of strengthening a party opposite to the public interest, ever happened to be motives in those advancements. What share of knowledge these Lords had in the laws of their country, and how they came by it, so as to enable them to decide the properties of their fellow-subjects in the last resort. Whether they were always so free from avarice, partialities, or want, that a bribe or some other sinister view, could have no place among them. Whether those holy Lords I spoke of were constantly promoted to that rank upon account of their knowledge in religious matters and the sanctity of their lives; had never been compliers with the times while they were common priests; or slavish prostitute chaplains to some nobleman, whose opinions they continued servilely to follow after they were admitted into that assembly.

He then desired to know what arts were practised in electing those whom I called commoners. Whether a stranger with a strong purse might not influence the vulgar voters to choose him before their own landlord, or the most considerable gentleman in the neighbourhood. How it came to pass, that people were so violently bent upon getting into this assembly, which I allowed to be great trouble and expense, often to the ruin of their families, without any salary or pension—because this appeared such an exalted strain of virtue and public spirit. His Majesty seemed to doubt it might possibly not be always sincere: and he desired to know whether such zealous gentlemen could have any views of refunding themselves for the charges and trouble they were at, by sacrificing the public good to the designs of a weak and vicious prince in conjunction with a corrupted ministry. He multiplied his questions, and sifted me thoroughly upon every part of this subject, proposing numberless enquiries and objections, which I think it not prudent or convenient to repeat.

He wondered to hear me talk of such chargeable and extensive wars; that certainly we must be a quarrelsome people, or live among very bad neighbours, and that our generals must needs be richer than our kings. He asked what business we had out of our own islands, unless upon the score of trade or treaty, or to defend the coasts with our fleet. Above all, he was amazed to hear me talk of a mercenary standing army in the midst of peace, and among a free people. He said, if we were governed by our own consent in the persons of our representatives, he could not imagine of whom we were afraid, or against whom we were to fight, and would hear my opinion, whether a private man's house might not better be defended by himself, his children, and family, than by half a dozen rascals picked up at a venture in the streets, for small wages, who might get an hundred times more by cutting their throats.

He was perfectly astonished with the historical account I gave him of our affairs during the last century, protesting it was only a heap of conspiracies, rebellions, murders, massacres, revolutions, banishments, and the very worst effects that avarice, faction, hypocrisy, perfidiousness, cruelty, rage, madness, hatred, envy, lust, malice, and ambition could produce.

His Majesty in another audience was at pains to recapitulate the sum of all I had spoken, compared the questions he made with the answers I had given; then taking me into his hands and stroking me gently, delivered himself in these words which I shall never forget, nor the manner he spoke them in. "My little friend, you have made a most admirable panegyric upon your country. You have clearly proved that ignorance, idleness, and vice are the proper ingredients for qualifying a legislator. That laws are best explained, interpreted, and applied by those whose interest and abilities lie in perverting, confounding, and eluding them. I observe among you some lines of an institution, which in its original might have been tolerable; but these half-erased, and the rest wholly blurred and blotted by corruptions. As for yourself who have spent the greatest part of your life in travelling, I am well disposed to hope you may hitherto have escaped many views of your country. But, by what I have gathered from your own relation, I cannot but conclude the bulk of your natives, to be the most pernicious race of little odious vermin that nature ever suffered to crawl upon the surface of the earth."

CHAPTER SEVEN

GULLIVER'S PROPOSAL IS REJECTED

Nothing but an extreme love of truth could have hindered me from concealing this part of my story. It was in vain to discover my resentments, which were always turned into ridicule; and I was forced to rest with patience while my noble and most beloved country was so injuriously treated. I am heartily sorry as any of my readers can possibly be, that such an occasion was given: but this Prince happened to be so curious and inquisitive upon every particular, that it could not consist either with gratitude or good manners to refuse giving him what satisfaction I was able. Yet this much I may be allowed to say in my own vindication, that I artfully eluded many of his questions, and gave to every point a more favourable turn by many degrees than the strictness of truth would allow.

Great allowances should be given to a King who lives wholly secluded from the rest of the world, and must therefore be altogether unacquainted with the manners and customs that most prevail in other nations: the want of which knowledge will ever produce many *prejudices*, and a certain *narrowness of thinking*, from which we and the politer countries of Europe are wholly exempted. And it would be hard indeed, if so remote a Prince's notions of virtue and vice were to be offered as a standard for all mankind.

To confirm what I have now said, and further, to show the miserable effects of a confined education, I shall here insert a passage which will hardly obtain belief. In hopes to ingratiate myself farther into His Majesty's favour, I told him of an invention discovered between three and four hundred years ago, to make a certain powder, into an heap of which the smallest spark of fire falling, would kindle the whole in a moment, although it were as big as a mountain, and make it all fly up in the air together, with a noise and agitation greater than thunder. That a proper quantity of this powder rammed into an hollow tube of brass or iron, according to its bigness, would drive a ball of iron or lead with such violence and speed as nothing was able to sustain its force. That the largest balls thus discharged, would not only destroy whole ranks of an army at once, but batter the strongest walls to the ground, sink down ships, with a thousand men in each, to the bottom of the sea; and when linked together by a chain, would cut through masts and rigging, divide hundreds of bodies in the middle, and lay all waste before them. That we often put this powder into large hollow balls of iron, and discharged them by an engine into some city we were besieging, which would rip up the pavements, tear the houses to pieces; burst and throw splinters on every side, dashing out the brains of all who came near. That I knew the ingredients very well, which were cheap and common; I understood the manner of compounding them, and could direct his workmen how to make those tubes of a size proportionable to all other things in His Majesty's kingdom, and the largest need not be above two hundred foot long; twenty or thirty of which tubes, charged with the proper quantity of powder and balls would batter down the walls of the strongest town in his dominions in a few hours, or destroy the whole metropolis, if ever it should pretend to dispute his absolute commands. This I humbly offered to His Majesty as a small tribute of acknowledgement in return of so many marks that I had received of his royal favour and protection.

The King was struck with horror at the description I had given of those terrible engines, and the proposal I had made. He was amazed how so impotent and grovelling an insect as I (these were his expressions) could entertain such inhuman ideas, and in so familiar a manner as to appear wholly unmoved at all the scenes of blood and desolation, which I had painted as the common effects of those destructive machines, whereof he said, some evil genius, enemy to mankind, must have been the first contriver. As for himself, he protested, that although few things delighted him so much as new discoveries in art or in nature, yet he would rather lose half his kingdom than be privy to such a secret, which he commended me, as I valued my life, never to mention any more.

A strange effect of *narrow principles* and *short views*, that a prince possessed of every quality which procures veneration, love, and esteem, of strong parts, great wisdom and profound learning, endued with admirable talents for government, and almost adored by his subjects, should form a *nice unnecessary scruple*, whereof in Europe we can have no conception, let slip an opportunity put into his hands that would have made him absolute master of the lives, the liberties and the fortunes of his people. Neither do I say this with the least intention to detract from the many virtues of that excellent King, whose character I am sensible will on this account be very much lessened in the opinion of an English reader; but I take this defect among them to have risen from their ignorance, by not having hitherto reduced *politics* into a *science*, as the more acute wits of Europe have done. For, I remember very well, in a discourse one day with the King, when I happened to say there were several thousand books among us written upon the *Art of Government*, it gave him (directly contrary to my intention) a very mean opinion of our understandings. He professed both to abominate and despise all *mystery*, *refinement*, and *intrigue*, either in a prince or a minister. He could not tell what I meant by *secrets of State*, where an enemy or some rival nation were not in the case. He confined the knowledge of governing within very *narrow bounds*; to common sense and reason, to justice and lenity, to the speedy determination of civil and criminal causes, with some other obvious topics which are not worth considering. And, he gave it for his opinion, that whoever could make two ears of corn, or two blades of grass grow upon a spot of ground where only one grew before, would deserve better of mankind, and do more essential service to his country, than the whole race of politicians put together.

CHAPTER EIGHT

GULLIVER RETURNS HOME

I had always a strong impulse that I should sometime recover my liberty, though it was impossible to conjecture by what means, or to form any project with the least hope of succeeding. The King was strongly bent to get me a woman of my own size, by whom I might propagate the breed: but I think I should rather have died than undergone the disgrace of leaving a posterity to be kept in cages like tame canary birds, and perhaps in time sold about the kingdom to persons of quality for curiosities. I was indeed treated with much kindness; I was the favourite of a great King and Queen, and the delight of the whole court, but it was upon such a foot as ill became the dignity of humankind. I could never forget those domestic pledges I had left behind me. I wanted to be among people with whom I could converse upon even terms, and walk about the streets and fields without fear of being trod to death like a frog or a young puppy. But, my deliverance came sooner than I expected, and in a manner not very common.

I had now been two years in this country, and about the beginning of the third, Glumdalclitch and I attended the King and Queen in a progress to the south coast of the kingdom.

When we came to our journey's end, the King thought proper to pass a few days at a palace by the seaside. Glumdalclitch and I were much fatigued; I had gotten a small cold, but the poor girl was so ill as to be confined to her chamber. I pretended to be worse than I really was, and desired leave to take the fresh air of the sea, with a page whom I was very fond of, and who had sometimes been trusted with me. I shall never forget with what unwillingness Glumdalclitch consented, nor the strict charge she gave the page to be careful of me, bursting at the same time into a flood of tears, as if she had some foreboding of what was to happen. The boy took me out in my box about half an hour's walk from the palace, towards the rocks on the seashore. I ordered him to set me down, and lifting up one of my sashes, cast many a wistful melancholy look towards the sea. I found myself not very well, and told the page that I had a mind to take a nap in my hammock, which I hoped would do me good. I got in, and the boy shut the window close down to keep out the cold. I soon fell asleep, and all I can conjecture is that while I slept, the page, thinking no danger could happen, went among the rocks to look for birds' eggs. I found myself suddenly awaked with a violent pull upon the ring which was fastened at the top of my box for the conveniency of carriage. I felt the box raised very high in the air, and then borne forward with prodigious speed. I called out several times as loud as I could raise my voice, but all to no purpose. I looked towards my windows, and could see nothing but the clouds and sky. I heard a noise just over my head like the clapping of wings, and then began to perceive the woeful condition I was in; that some eagle had got the ring of my box in his beak, with an intent to let it fall on a rock like a tortoise in a shell, and then pick out my body and devour it.

In a little time, all of a sudden I felt myself falling perpendicularly down for above a minute, but with much incredible swiftness that I almost lost my breath. My fall was stopped by a terrible squash. I now perceived that I was fallen into the sea. My box, by the weight of my body, the goods that were in it, and the broad plates of iron fixed for strength at the four corners of the top and bottom, floated about five foot deep in water. I did then, and do now suppose that the eagle which flew away with my box was pursued by two or three others, and forced to let me drop while he was defending himself against the rest, who hoped to share in the prey. The plates of iron fastened at the bottom of the box preserved the balance while it fell, and hindered it from being broken on the surface of the water. How often did I then wish myself with my dear Glumdalclitch, from whom one single hour had so far divided me! And I may say with truth, that in the midst of my own misfortunes I could not forbear lamenting my poor nurse, the grief she would suffer for my loss, the displeasure of the Queen, and the ruin of her fortune.

Being in this disconsolate state, I heard or at least thought I heard some kind of grating noise on the side of my box, and soon after, I began to fancy that the box was pulled, or towed along in the sea. I ventured to unscrew one of my chairs, which were always fastened to the floor; and having made a hard shift to screw it down again directly under the slipping-board that I had lately opened, I mounted on the chair, and putting my mouth as near as I could to the hole, I called for help in a loud voice, and in all the languages I understood. I then fastened my handkerchief to a stick I usually carried, and thrusting it up the hole, waved it several times in the air, that if any boat or ship were near, the seamen might conjecture some unhappy mortal to be shut up in the box.

I plainly heard a noise upon the cover of my closet, like that of a cable, and the grating of it as it passed through the ring. I then found myself hoisted up by degrees at least three foot higher than I was before. Whereupon, I again thrust up my stick and handkerchief, calling for help till I was almost hoarse. In return to which, I heard a great shout repeated three times, giving me such transport of joy as is not to be conceived but by those who feel them. I now heard a trampling over my head, and somebody calling through the hole with a loud voice in the English tongue: *If there be anybody below let them speak*. I answered I was an Englishman, drawn by ill fortune into the greatest calamity that ever any creature underwent, and begged, by all that was moving, to be delivered out of the dungeon I was in. The voice replied I was safe, for my box was fastened to their ship, and the carpenter should immediately come, and saw a hole in the cover, large enough to pull me out. I answered, that was needless, and would take up too much time, for there was no more to be done, but let one of the crew put his finger into the ring, and take the box out of the sea into the ship, and so into the captain's cabin. Some of them upon hearing me talk so wildly, thought I was mad. Others laughed; for indeed it never came into my head that I was now among people of my own stature and strength. The carpenter came, and in a few minutes sawed a passage about four foot square, then let down a small ladder upon which I mounted, and from thence was taken into the ship in a very weak condition.

The sailors were all in amazement, and asked me a thousand questions, which I had no inclination to answer. I was equally confounded at the sight of so many pygmies, for such I took them to be, after having so long accustomed mine eyes to the monstrous objects I had left. But the captain, Mr Thomas Wilcocks, an honest worthy Shropshire man, observing I was ready to faint, took me into his cabin, gave me a cordial to comfort me, and made me turn in upon his own bed, advising me to take a little rest, of which I had great need.

I slept some hours, but perpetually disturbed with dreams of the place I had left, and the dangers I had escaped. However, upon waking I found myself much recovered. The captain ordered supper immediately, thinking I had already fasted too long. He entertained me with great kindness, observing me not to look wildly, or talk inconsistently; and when we were left alone, desired I would give him a relation of my travels, and by what accident I came to be set adrift in that monstrous wooden chest.

I begged his patience to hear me tell my story, which I faithfully did from the last time I left England to the moment he first discovered me. This honest worthy gentleman, who had some tincture of learning, and very good sense, was immediately convinced of my candour and veracity. But, further to confirm all I had said, I entreated him to give order that my cabinet should be brought, of which I had the key in my pocket. I opened it in his presence, and showed him the small collection of rarities I made in the country from whence I had been so strangely delivered. There was the comb I had contrived out of the stumps of the King's beard, and a gold ring which one day the Queen made me a present of in a most obliging manner, taking it from her little finger, and throwing it over my head like a collar. I desired the captain would please to accept this ring in return of his civilities, which he absolutely refused. Lastly, I desired him to see the breeches I had then on, which were made of a mouse's skin.

I could force nothing on him but a footman's tooth, which I observed him to examine with great curiosity, and found he had a fancy for it. He received it with abundance of thanks, more than such a trifle could deserve. It was drawn by an unskilful surgeon in a mistake from one of Glumdalclitch's men, who was afflicted with the toothache, but it was as sound as any in his head. I got it cleaned, and put it into my cabinet. It was about a foot long, and four inches in diameter.

The captain was very well satisfied with this plain relation I had given him, and said he hoped when we returned to England, I would oblige the world by putting it on paper, and making it public. I thanked him for his good opinion, and promised to take the matter into my thoughts.

Our voyage was very prosperous. The captain called in at one or two ports and sent in his long-boat for provisions and fresh water, but I never went out of the ship till we came into the Downs, which was on the 3rd day of June, 1706, about nine months after my escape. I offered to leave my goods in security for payment of my freight, but the captain protested he would not receive one farthing. We took kind leave of each other, and I made him promise he would come to see me at my house.

As I was on the road, observing the littleness of the houses, the trees, the cattle and the people, I began to think myself in Lilliput. I was afraid of trampling on every traveller I met, and often called aloud to have them stand out of the way, so that I had like to have gotten one or two broken heads for my impertinence.

When I came to my own house, for which I was forced to enquire, one of the servants opening the door, I bent down to go in (like a goose under a gate) for fear of striking my head.

My wife ran out to embrace me, but I stooped lower than her knees, thinking she could otherwise never be able to reach my mouth. My daughter kneeled to ask me blessing, but I could not see her till she arose, having been so long used to stand with my head and eyes erect to above sixty feet. I looked down upon the servants and one or two friends who were in the house, as if they were pygmies, and I a giant. In short, I behaved so unaccountably, that they were all of the captain's opinion when he first saw me, and concluded I had lost my wits. This I mention as an instance of the great power of habit and prejudice.

PART III: A VOYAGE TO LAPUTA, BALNIBARBI, LUGGNAGG, GLUBBDUBDRIB AND JAPAN

CHAPTER ONE: GULLIVER ARRIVES IN LAPUTA

I had not been at home above ten days when Captain William Robinson, a Cornish man, commander of the *Hope-well,* invited me to be surgeon of the ship. We set out the 5th day of August, 1706, and arrived at Fort St George, the 11th of April, 1707. We stayed there three weeks to refresh our crew. From thence we went to Tonquin, where the captain, having business there, resolved to continue some time. In hopes to defray some of the charges he must be at, he bought a sloop, loaded it with several sorts of goods, appointed me master of the sloop, and gave me power to traffic while he transacted his affairs.

We had not sailed above three days when, a great storm arising, we were driven five days to the north-north-east, and then to the east, after which we had fair weather, but still with a pretty strong gale from the west. Upon the tenth day, we were chased by two pirates who soon overtook us.

We were boarded about the same time by both the pirates, who entered furiously at the head of their men, but finding us all prostrate upon our faces (for so I gave order), they pinioned us with strong ropes, and set a guard upon us.

I observed among them a Dutchman, who seemed to be of some authority, though he was not commander of either ship. He knew us by our countenances to be Englishmen, and jabbering to us in his own language, swore we should be tied back to back, and thrown into the sea. I spoke Dutch tolerably well; I told him who we were, and begged him in consideration of our being Christians and Protestants of neighbouring countries in strict alliance, that he would move the captains to take some pity on us. This inflamed his rage, he repeated his threatenings, and turning to his companions, spoke with great vehemence in the Japanese language, as I suppose, often using the word *Christianos.*

The larger of the two pirate ships was commanded by a Japanese captain, who spoke a little Dutch, but very imperfectly. He came up to me, and after several questions, which I answered in great humility, he said we should not die. I made the captain a very low bow, and then turning to the Dutchman, said, I was sorry to find more mercy in a heathen, than in a brother Christian. But I had soon reason to repent those foolish words, for that malicious reprobate, having often endeavoured in vain to persuade both the captains that I might be thrown into the sea (which they would not yield to after the promise made me, that I should not die), however prevailed so far as to have a punishment inflicted on me, worse in all human appearance than death itself. My men were sent by an equal division into both the pirate ships. As to myself, it was determined that I should be set adrift, in a small canoe, with paddles and a sail, and four days' provisions, which last the Japanese captain was so kind to double out of his own stores, and would permit no man to search me. I got down into the canoe, while the Dutchman, standing upon the deck, loaded me with all the curses and injurious terms his language could afford.

When I was at some distance from the pirates, I discovered by my pocket-glass several islands to the south-east. I set up my sail, the wind being fair, with a design to reach the nearest of those islands, which I made a shift to do in about three hours. It was all rocky; however I got many birds' eggs, and, striking fire, I kindled some dry grass and seaweed, by which I roasted my eggs. I ate no other supper, being resolved to spare my provisions as much as I could. I passed the night under the shelter of a cave, strewing some heath under me, and slept pretty well.

The next day I sailed to another island, and thence to a third and fourth. On the fifth day I arrived at the last island in my sight. This island was at a greater distance than I expected, and I did not reach it in less than five hours. I considered how impossible it was to preserve my life in so desolate a place, and how miserable my end must be. I walked a while among the rocks; the sky was perfectly clear, and the sun so hot that I was forced to turn my face from it: when all of a sudden it became obscured, as I thought, in a manner very different from what happens by the interposition of a cloud.

I turned back, and perceived a vast opaque body between me and the sun, moving forwards towards the island: it seemed to be about two miles high, and hid the sun six or seven minutes, but I did not observe the air to be much colder, or the sky more darkened, than if I had stood under the shade of a mountain. As it approached nearer over the place where I was, it appeared to be a firm substance, the bottom flat, smooth, and shining very bright from the reflection of the sea below. I stood upon a height about two hundred yards from the shore, and saw this vast body descending almost to a parallel with me, at less than an English mile's distance. I took out my pocket-perspective, and could plainly discover numbers of people moving up and down the sides of it, which appeared to be sloping, but what those people were doing, I was not able to distinguish.

The reader can hardly conceive my astonishment to behold an island in the air. It advanced nearer, and I could see the sides of it encompassed with several gradations of galleries and stairs, at certain intervals, to descend from one to the other. Upon its nearer approach, I called with the utmost strength of my voice; a crowd gathered to that side which was most in my view. In less than half an hour, the island was moved and raised in such a manner, that the lowest gallery appeared in a parallel of less than an hundred yards' distance from the height where I stood. I then put myself into the most supplicating postures, and spoke in the humblest accent, but received no answer. Those who stood nearest over against me, seemed to be persons of distinction, as I supposed by their habit. They conferred earnestly with each other, looking often upon me. At length one of them called out in a clear, polite, smooth dialect, not unlike in sound to the Italian; and therefore I returned an answer in that language, hoping at least that the cadence might be more agreeable to his ears. Although neither of us understood the other, yet my meaning was easily known, for the people saw the distress I was in.

They made signs for me to come down from the rock, and go towards the shore, which I accordingly did; and the flying island being raised to a convenient height, the verge directly over me, a chain was let down from the lowest gallery, with a seat fastened to the bottom, to which I fixed myself, and was drawn up by pulleys.

CHAPTER TWO

THE LAPUTANS

At my alighting I was surrounded by a crowd of people, but those who stood nearest seemed to be of better quality. They beheld me with all the marks and circumstances of wonder, neither indeed was I much in their debt, having never till then seen a race of mortals so singular in their shapes, habits and countenances. Their heads were all reclined either to the right, or the left; one of their eyes turned inward, and the other directly up to the zenith. Their outward garments were adorned with the figures of suns, moons, and stars, interwoven with those of fiddles, flutes, harps, trumpets, guitars, harpsichords, and many more instruments of music, unknown to us in Europe. I observed here and there, many in the habit of servants, with a blown bladder fastened like a flail to the end of a short stick, which they carried in their hands. In each bladder was a small quantity of dried peas or little pebbles (as I was afterwards informed). With these bladders, they now and then flapped the mouths and ears of those who stood near them. It seems the minds of these people are so taken up with intense speculations that they neither can speak, nor attend to the discourses of others without being roused by some external taction upon the organs of speech and hearing; for which reason, those persons who are able to afford it always keep a *flapper* in their family, as one of their domestics, and never walk abroad or make visits without him. And the business of this officer is, when two or more persons are in company, gently to strike with his bladder, the mouth of him who is to speak, and the right ear of him or them to whom the speaker addresseth himself. This flapper is likewise employed diligently to attend his master in his walks, and upon occasion to give him a soft flap on his eyes, because he is always so wrapped up in cogitation, that he is in manifest danger of falling down every precipice, and bounding his head against every post, and in the streets, of jostling others or being jostled himself into the kennel.

At last we entered the palace, and proceeded into the chamber of presence, where I saw the King seated on his throne, attended on each side by persons of prime quality. Before the throne, was a large table filled with globes and spheres, and mathematical instruments of all kinds. His Majesty took not the least notice of us, although our entrance was not without sufficient noise, by the concourse of all persons belonging to the Court. But, he was then deep in a problem, and we attended at least an hour, before he could solve it. There stood by him on each side, a young page, with flaps in their hands and when they saw he was at leisure, one of them gently struck his mouth, and the other his right ear, at which he started like one awaked all of a sudden and looking towards me, and the company I was in, recollected the occasion of our coming, whereof he had been informed before. He spoke some words, whereupon immediately a young man with a flap came up to my side, and flapped me gently on the right ear. But I made signs as well as I could, that I had no occasion for such an instrument; which as I afterwards found, gave His Majesty and the whole Court a very mean opinion of my understanding. The King, as far as I could conjecture, asked me several questions, and I addressed myself to him in all the languages I knew. When it was found that I could neither understand nor be understood, I was conducted by his order to an apartment in his palace. My dinner was brougnt, and four persons of quality, whom I remembered to have seen very near the King's person, did me the honour to dine with me.

A person was sent by the King's order to teach me the language. When I went next to Court, I was able to understand many things the King spoke, and to return him some kind of answers. His

Majesty had given orders that the island should move north-east to the vertical point over Lagado, the metropolis of the whole kingdom below upon the firm earth.

In our journey towards Lagado the capital city, His Majesty ordered that the island should stop over certain towns and villages, from whence he might receive the petitions of his subjects. And to this purpose, several pack-threads were let down with small weights at the bottom. On these pack-threads the people strung their petitions, which mounted up directly like the scraps of paper fastened by schoolboys at the end of the string that holds their kite. Sometimes we received wine and victuals from below, which were drawn up by pulleys.

The people of this island are under continual disquietudes, never enjoying a minute's peace of mind; and their disturbances proceed from causes which very little affect the rest of mortals. Their apprehensions arise from several changes they dread in the celestial bodies. For instance, that the earth by the continual approaches of the sun towards it, must in course of time be absorbed or swallowed up. That the face of the sun will by degrees be encrusted with its own effluvia, and give no more light to the world. That the earth very narrowly escaped a brush from the tail of the last comet, which would have infallibly reduced it to ashes; and that the sun, daily spending its rays without any nutriment to supply them, will at last be wholly consumed and annihilated; which must be attended with the destruction of this earth, and of all the planets that receive their light from it.

They are so perpetually alarmed with the apprehensions of these and the like impending dangers, that they can neither sleep quietly in their beds, nor have any relish for the common pleasures or amusements of life. When they meet an acquaintance in the morning, the first question is about the sun's health, how he looked at his setting and rising, and what hopes they have to avoid the stroke of the approaching comet. This conversation they are apt to run into with the same temper that boys discover, in delighting to hear terrible stories of spirits and hobgoblins, which they greedily listen to, and dare not go to bed for fear.

CHAPTER THREE

THE MONARCH OF LAPUTA

The Flying or Floating Island (in the original, *Laputa)* is exactly circular, its diameter 7,837 yards, or about four miles and an half, and consequently contains ten thousand acres. It is three hundred yards thick. The bottom or under-surface, which appears to those who view it from below, is one even regular plate of adamant, shooting up to the height of about two hundred yards. The greatest curiosity, upon which the fate of the island depends, is a lodestone of a prodigious size, in shape resembling a weaver's shuttle. By means of this lodestone, the island is made to rise and fall, and move from one place to another. For, with respect to that part of the earth over which the monarch presides, the stone is endued at one of its sides with an attractive power, and at the other with a repulsive. Upon placing the magnet erect with its attracting end towards the earth, the island descends; but when the repelling extremity points downwards, the island mounts directly upwards. When the position of the stone is oblique, the motion of the island is so too. For in this magnet, the forces always act in lines parallel to its direction. By this oblique motion the island is conveyed to different parts of the monarch's dominions. But it must be observed that this island cannot move beyond the extent of the dominions below, nor can it rise above the height of four miles.

The King would be the most absolute prince in the universe, if he could but prevail on a Ministry to join with him; but these having their estates below on the continent, would never consent to the enslaving of their country.

If any town should engage in rebellion or mutiny, fall into violent factions, or refuse to pay the usual tribute, the King hath two methods of reducing them to obedience. The first and the mildest course is by keeping the island hovering over such a town, and the lands about it, whereby he can deprive them of the benefit of the sun and the rain, and consequently afflict the inhabitants with dearth and diseases. And if the crime deserve it, they are at the same time pelted from above with great stones, against which they have no defence, but to creep into cellars or caves, while the roofs of their houses are beaten to pieces. But if they still continue obstinate, or offer to raise insurrections, he proceeds to the last remedy, by letting the island drop directly upon their heads, which makes a universal destruction both of houses and men. However, this is an extremity to which the Prince is seldom driven, neither indeed is he willing to put it in execution, nor dare his Ministers advise him to such an action which would render them odious to the people, and be a great damage to their own estates that lie all below.

CHAPTER FOUR

GULLIVER IS RECEIVED BY A GREAT LORD

Although I cannot say that I was ill-treated in this island, yet I must confess I thought myself too much neglected, not without some degree of contempt. For neither Prince nor people appeared to be curious in any part of knowledge, except mathematics and music, wherein I was far their inferior, and upon that account, very little regarded. They were indeed excellent in two sciences for which I have great esteem, and wherein I am not unversed, but at the same time, so abstracted and involved in speculation that I never met with such disagreeable companions. I conversed only with women, tradesmen, flappers, and court-pages during two months of my abode there, by which at least I rendered myself extremely contemptible, yet these were the only people from whom I could ever receive a reasonable answer.

There was a great lord at court, nearly related to the King, and for that reason alone, used with respect. He was universally reckoned the most ignorant and stupid person among them. I entreated this illustrious person to intercede on my behalf with His Majesty for leave to depart, which he accordingly did.

On the 16th day of February, I took leave of His Majesty and the court. The King made me a present to the value of about two hundred English pounds, and my protector, his kinsman, as much more, together with a letter of recommendation to a friend of his in Lagado, the metropolis; the island being then hovering over a mountain about two miles from it, I was let down from the lowest gallery, in the same manner as I had been taken up.

The continent, as far as it is subject to the monarch of the Flying Island, passeth under the general name of Balnibarbi, and the metropolis, as I said before, is called Lagado. I felt some little satisfaction in finding myself on firm ground. I walked to the city without any concern, being clad like one of the natives, and sufficiently instructed to converse with them. I soon found out the person's house to whom I was recommended, presented my letter from his friend the grandee in the island, and was received with much kindness. This great lord ordered me an apartment in his own house, where I continued during my stay, and was entertained in a most hospitable manner.

The morning after my arrival, he took me in his chariot to see the town, which is about half the bigness of London, but the houses very strangely built, and most of them out of repair. The people in the streets walked fast, looked wild, their eyes fixed, and were generally in rags. He said if I would go with him to his country house, about twenty miles distant, where his estate lay, there would be more leisure for conversation. I told his Excellency that I was entirely at his disposal, and accordingly we set out next morning.

During our journey, he made me observe the several methods used by farmers in managing their lands, which to me were wholly unaccountable, for except in a few places, I could not discover one ear of corn or blade of grass. But, in three hours travelling, the scene was wholly altered; we came into a most beautiful country; farmers' houses at small distances, neatly built, the fields enclosed, containing vineyards, corn-grounds and meadows. Neither do I remember to have seen a more delightful prospect. His Excellency observed my countenance to clear up; he told me with a sigh, that there his estate began, and would continue the same till we should come to his house. That his countrymen ridiculed and despised him for managing his affairs no better, and for setting so ill an example to the kingdom, which however was followed by very few, such as were old and wilful and weak like himself.

We came at length to the house which was indeed a noble structure, built according to the best rules of ancient architecture. The fountains, gardens, walks, avenues, and groves were all disposed with exact judgment and taste. I gave due praises to everything I saw, whereof His Excellency took not the least notice till after supper, when, there being no third companion, he told me with a very melancholy air, that he doubted he must throw down his houses in town and country, to rebuild them after the present mode, destroy all his plantations, and cast others into such a form as modern usage required, and give the same directions to all his tenants, unless he would submit to incur the censure of pride, singularity, affectation, ignorance, caprice, and perhaps increase His Majesty's displeasure.

About forty years ago, certain persons went up to Laputa either upon business or diversion, and after five months' continuance, came back with a smattering in mathematics, but full of volatile spirits acquired in that airy region. These persons upon their return began to dislike the management of everything below, and fell into schemes of putting all arts, sciences, languages, and mechanics upon a new foot. To this end they procured a royal patent for erecting an Academy of Projectors in Lagado; and this humour prevailed so strongly among the people, that there is not a town of any consequence in the kingdom without such an Academy. In these colleges, the professors contrive new rules and methods of agriculture and building, and new instruments and tools for all trades and manufactures, whereby, as they undertake, one man shall do the work of ten; a palace may be built in a week, of materials so durable as to last for ever without repairing. All the fruits of the earth shall come to maturity at whatever season we think fit to choose, and increase an hundredfold more than they do at present, with innumerable other happy proposals. The only inconvenience is that none of these projects are yet brought to perfection, and in the meantime the whole country lies miserably waste, the houses in ruins, and the people without food or clothes.

In a few days we came back to town, and His Excellency resolved I should certainly view the grand academy. Considering the bad character he had in the Academy, he would not go with me himself, but recommended me to a friend of his to bear me company thither.

CHAPTER FIVE

THE GRAND ACADEMY OF LAGADO

I was received very kindly by the warden, and went for many days to the Academy. Every room hath in it one or more Projectors, and I believe I could not be in fewer than five hundred rooms.

The first man I saw was of a meagre aspect, with sooty hands and face, his hair and beard long, ragged and singed in several places. His clothes, shirt, and skin were all of the same colour. He had been eight years upon a project for extracting sunbeams out of cucumbers, which were to be put into vials hermetically sealed, and let out to warm the air in raw inclement summers. He told me, he did not doubt in eight years more, that he should be able to supply the Governor's gardens with sunshine at a reasonable rate; but he complained that his stock was low, and entreated me to give him something as an encouragement to ingenuity, especially since this had been a very dear season for cucumbers. I made him a small present, for my Lord had furnished me with money on purpose, because he knew their practice of begging from all who go to see them.

I went into another chamber, but was ready to hasten back, being almost overcome with a horrible stink. My conductor pressed me forward, conjuring me in a whisper to give no offence, which would be highly resented, and therefore I durst not so much as stop my nose. The projector of this cell was the most ancient student of the Academy. His face and beard were of a pale yellow; his hands and clothes daubed over with filth. When I was presented to him, he gave me a very close embrace (a compliment I could well have excused). His employment from his first coming into the Academy was an operation to reduce human excrement to its original food, by separating the several parts, removing the tincture which it receives from the gall, making the odour exhale, and scumming off the saliva. He had a weekly allowance from the Society of a vessel filled with human ordure, about the bigness of a Bristol barrel.

I saw another at work to calcine ice into gunpowder, who likewise showed me a treatise he had written concerning the malleability of fire, which he intended to publish.

There was a most ingenious architect who had contrived a new method for building houses; by beginning at the roof and working downwards to the foundation, which he justified to me by the like practice of those two prudent insects, the bee and the spider.

There was a man born blind, who had several apprentices in his own condition; their employment was to mix colours for painters, which their master taught them to distinguish by feeling and smelling. It was indeed my misfortune to find them at that time not very perfect in their lessons, and the professor himself happened to be generally mistaken: this artist is much encouraged and esteemed by the whole fraternity.

In another apartment I was highly pleased with a projector, who had found a device of ploughing the ground with hogs, to save the charges of ploughs, cattle, and labour. The method is this: in an acre of ground you bury, at six inches distance, and eight deep, a quantity of acorns, dates, chestnuts, or vegetables whereof these animals are fondest: then you drive six hundred or more of them into the field, wherein a few days they will root up the whole ground in search of their food, and make it fit for sowing, at the same time manuring it with their dung. It is true upon experiment they found the charge and trouble very great, and they had little or no crop. However, it is not doubted that this invention may be capable of great improvement.

I went into another room, where the walls and ceiling were all hung round with cobwebs, except a narrow passage for the artist to go in and out. At my entrance he called aloud to me not to disturb his webs. He lamented the fatal mistake the world had been so long in of using silkworms, while we had such plenty of domestic insects, who infinitely excelled the former, because they understood how to weave as well as spin. And he proposed farther, that by employing spiders, the charge of dyeing silks would be wholly saved, whereof I was fully convinced when he showed me a vast number of flies most beautifully coloured, wherewith he fed his spiders, assuring us, that the webs would take a tincture from them; and as he had them of all hues, he hoped to fit everybody's fancy, as soon as he could find proper food for the flies, of certain gums, oils, and other glutinous matter to give a strength and consistence to the threads.

We crossed a walk to the other part of the Academy, where the projectors in speculative learning resided.

I was at the mathematical school, where the master taught his pupils after a method scarce imaginable to us in Europe. The proposition and demonstration were fairly written on a thin wafer, with ink composed of a cephalic tincture. This the student was to swallow upon a fasting stomach, and for three days following eat nothing but bread and water. As the wafer digested, the tincture mounted to his brain, bearing the proposition along with it. But the success hath not hitherto been answerable, partly by some error in the quantum or composition, and partly by the perverseness of lads, to whom this bolus is so nauseous that they generally steal aside, and discharge it upwards before it can operate; neither have they been yet persuaded to use so long an abstinence as the prescription requires.

CHAPTER SIX

A SHORT VOYAGE TO GLUBBDUBDRIB

I saw nothing in this country that could invite me to a longer continuance, and began to think of returning home to England. I hired two mules with a guide to show me the way, and carry my small baggage. I took leave of my noble protector, who had shown me so much favour, and made me a generous present at my departure. I set out for the great island of Luggnagg.

My journey was without any accident or adventure worth relating. When I arrived at the port of Maldonada there was no ship in the harbour bound for Luggnagg, nor like to be in some time. A gentleman of distinction said to me that since the ships bound for Luggnagg could not be ready in less than a month, it might be no disagreeable amusement for me to take a trip to the little island of Glubbdubdrib, about five leagues off to the south-west. He offered himself and a friend to accompany me.

Glubbdubdrib, as nearly as I can interpret the word, signifies the Island of Sorcerers or Magicians. It is about one third as large as the Isle of Wight, and extremely fruitful: it is governed by the head of a certain tribe, who are all magicians. This tribe marries only among each other, and the eldest in succession is Prince or Governor.

The Governor and his family are served and attended by domestics of a kind somewhat unusual. By his skill in necromancy, he hath power of calling whom he pleaseth from the dead, and commanding their service for twenty-four hours, but no longer nor can he call the same persons up again in less than three months, except upon very extraordinary occasions. The Governor ordered me to call up whatever persons I would choose to name, and in whatever numbers, among all the dead from the beginning of the world to the present time, and command them to answer any questions I should think fit to ask.

Having a desire to see those ancients who were most renowned for wit and learning, I proposed that Homer and Aristotle might appear at the head of all their commentators. I knew and could distinguish those two heroes at first sight, not only from the crowd, but from each other. Homer was the taller and comelier person of the two, walked very erect for one of his age, and his eyes were the most quick and piercing I ever beheld. Aristotle stooped much, and made use of a staff. His visage was meagre, his hair lank and thin, and his voice hollow. I soon discovered that both of them were perfect strangers to the rest of the company, and had never seen or heard of them before. And I had a whisper from a ghost, who shall be nameless, that these commentators always kept in the most distant quarters from their principals in the lower world, through a consciousness of shame and guilt, because they had so horribly misrepresented the meaning of those authors to posterity.

Vast numbers of illustrious persons were called up to gratify that insatiable desire I had to see the world in every period of antiquity placed before me. I chiefly fed my eyes with beholding kings, dukes, generals, courtiers, and many others. As every person called up made exactly the same appearance he had done in the world, it gave me melancholy reflections to observe how much the race of human kind was degenerate among us within these hundred years past; how the pox under all its consequences and denominations had altered every lineament of an English countenance, shortened the size of bodies, unbraced the nerves, relaxed the sinews and muscles, introduced a sallow complexion, and rendered the flesh loose and rancid.

I descended so low as to desire that some English yeomen of the old stamp might be summoned to appear, once so famous for the simplicity of their manners, diet and dress, for justice in their dealings, for their true spirit of liberty, for their valour and love of their country. Neither could I be wholly unmoved after comparing the living with the dead, when I considered how all these pure native virtues were prostituted for a piece of money by their grandchildren, who in selling their votes, and managing at elections, have acquired every vice and corruption that can possibly be learned in a Court.

CHAPTER SEVEN

THE IMMORTALS OF LUGGNAGG

The day of our departure being come, I took leave of his Highness the Governor of Glubbdubdrib, and returned with my two companions of Maldonada, where a ship was ready to sail for Luggnagg. The two gentlemen and some others were so generous and kind as to furnish me with provisions, and see me on board. I was a month in this voyage. We had one violent storm, and were under a necessity of steering westward to get into the trade wind, which holds for above sixty leagues. We cast anchor within a league of the town, and made a signal for a pilot. Two of them came on board in less than half an hour, by whom we were guided between certain shoals and rocks, which are very dangerous in the passage, to a large basin, where a fleet may ride in safety within a cable's length of the town wall.

Some of our sailors whether out of treachery or inadvertence, had informed the pilots that I was a stranger and a great traveller, whereof these gave notice to a custom-house officer, by whom I was examined very strictly upon my landing. This officer spoke to me in the language of Balnibarbi, which by the force of much commerce is generally understood in that town, especially by seamen, and those employed in the customs. I gave him a short account of some particulars, and made my story as plausible and consistent as I could; but I thought it necessary to disguise my country, and call myself a Hollander; because my intentions were for Japan, and I knew the Dutch were the only Europeans permitted to enter into that kingdom. I therefore told the officer, that having been shipwrecked on the coast of Balnibarbi, and cast on a rock, I was received up into Laputa, or the Flying Island (of which he had often heard) and was now endeavouring to get to Japan, from whence I might find a convenience of returning to my own country. The officer said I must be confined till he could receive orders from Court, for which he would write immediately, and hoped to receive an answer in a fortnight. I was carried to a convenient lodging, with a sentry placed at the door; however I had the liberty of a large garden, and was treated with humanity enough, being maintained all the time at the King's charge. I was visited by several persons, chiefly out of curiosity, because it was reported I came from countries very remote, of which they had never heard.

I hired a young man who came in the same ship to be an interpreter; he was a native of Luggnagg, but had lived some years at Maldonada, and was a perfect master of both languages. By his assistance I was able to hold a conversation with those that came to visit me; but this consisted only of their questions, and my answers.

The dispatch came from Court about the time we expected. It contained a warrant for conducting me and my retinue to Traldragdubh. All my retinue was that poor lad for an interpreter, whom I persuaded into my service. At my humble request we had each of us a mule to ride on. A messenger was dispatched half a day's journey before us, to give the King notice of my approach, and to desire that his Majesty would please to appoint a day and hour, when it would be his gracious pleasure that I might have the honour to *lick the dust before his footstool*. This is the Court style, and I found it to be more than matter of form.

The Luggnaggians are a polite and generous people, and although they are not without some share of that pride which is peculiar to all Eastern countries, yet they show themselves courteous to strangers, especially such who are countenanced by the court.

One day I was asked by a person of quality, whether I had seen any of their Struldbruggs or Immortals. I said I had not, and desired he would explain to me what he meant by such an appellation applied to a mortal creature. He told me that sometimes, though very rarely, a child happened to be born in a family with a red circular spot in the forehead, directly over the left eyebrow, which was an infallible mark that it should never die. The spot in the course of time grew larger, and changed its colour; for at twelve years old it became green, so continued till five and twenty, then turned to a deep blue; at five and forty it grew coal black, and as large as an English shilling, but never admitted any further alteration. He said these births were so rare, that he did not believe there could be above eleven hundred Struldbruggs of both sexes in the whole kingdom.

I freely own myself to have been struck with inexpressible delight upon hearing this account; and the person who gave it me happening to understand the Balnibarbian language, which I spoke very well, I could not forbear breaking out into expressions perhaps a little too extravagant. I cried out as in a rapture: Happy nation where every child hath at least a chance for being immortal. Happy people who enjoy so many living examples of ancient virtue, and have masters ready to instruct them in the wisdom of all former ages! But happiest beyond all comparison are those excellent Struldbruggs, who being born exempt from that universal calamity of human nature, have their minds free and disengaged, without the weight and depression of spirits caused by the continual apprehension of death.

The gentleman to whom I addressed my discourse, because he spoke the language of Balnibarbi, said to me with a sort of a smile, which usually ariseth from pity to the ignorant, that his friends and mine were very much pleased with the judicious remarks I had made on the great happiness and advantages of immortal life, and they were desirous to know in a particular manner, what scheme of living I should have formed to myself, if it had fallen to my lot to have been born a Struldbrugg.

I answered, that if it had been my good fortune to come into the world a Struldbrugg, I would first resolve by all arts and methods whatsoever to procure myself riches. I would from my earliest youth apply myself to the study of arts and sciences, by which I should arrive in time to excel all others in learning. By all which acquirements, I should be a living treasury of knowledge and wisdom, and certainly become the oracle of the nation.

I enlarged upon many other topics which the natural desire of endless life and sublunary happiness could easily furnish me with. When I had ended, and the sum of my discourse had been interpreted as before, to the rest of the company, there was a good deal of talk among them in the language of the country, not without some laughter at my expense. At last the same gentleman who had been my interpreter said, he was desired by the rest to set me right in a few mistakes, which I had fallen into through the common imbecility of human nature. That this breed of Struldbruggs was peculiar to their country. That whoever had one foot in the grave, was sure to hold back the other as strongly as he could. That the oldest had still hopes of living one day longer, and looked on death as the greatest evil, from which Nature always prompted him to retreat; only in this island of Luggnagg, the appetite for living was not so eager, from the continual example of the Struldbruggs before their eyes.

That the system of living contrived by me was unreasonable and unjust, because it supposed a perpetuity of youth, health, and vigour, which no man could be so foolish to hope, however extravagant he might be in his wishes. That the question therefore was not whether a man would choose to be always in the prime of youth, attended with prosperity and health, but how he would pass a perpetual life under all the usual disadvantages which old age brings along with it.

After this preface he gave me a particular account of Struldbruggs among them. He said they commonly acted like mortals, till about thirty years old, after which by degrees they grew melancholy and dejected, increasing in both till they came to fourscore. When they came to fourscore years, they had not only all the follies and infirmities of other old men, but many more which arose from the dreadful prospect of never dying. They were not only opinionative, peevish, covetous, morose, vain, talkative, but uncapable of friendship, and dead to all natural affection, which never descended below their grandchildren. Envy and impotent desires are their prevailing passions. But those objects against which their envy seems principally directed, are the vices of the younger sort, and the deaths of the old. By reflecting on the former, they find themselves cut off from all possibility of pleasure; and whenever they see a funeral, they lament and repine that others are gone to an harbour of rest, to which they themselves never can hope to arrive. They have no remembrance of anything. And for the truth or particulars of any fact, it is safer to depend on common traditions than upon their best recollections. The least miserable among them appear to be those who turn to dotage, and entirely lose their memories; these meet with more pity and assistance.

As soon as they completed the term of eighty years, they are looked on as dead in law; their heirs immediately succeed to their estates, only a small pittance is reserved for their support, and the poor ones are maintained at the public charge. After that period they are held incapable of any employment of trust or profit.

At ninety they lose their teeth and hair, they have at that age no distinction of taste, but eat and drink whatever they can get, without relish or appetite. They never can amuse themselves with reading, because their memory will not serve to carry them from the beginning of a sentence to the end; and by this defect they are deprived of the only entertainment whereof they might otherwise be capable.

This was the account given me of the Struldbruggs, I afterwards saw five or six of different ages, the youngest not above two hundred years old, who were brought to me at several times by some of my friends; but although they were told that I was a great traveller, and had seen all the world, they had not the least curiosity to ask me a question; only desired I would give them a token of remembrance, which is a modest way of begging.

They are despised and hated by all sorts of people; when one of them is born, it is reckoned ominous, and their birth is recorded very particularly. They were the most mortifying sight I ever beheld, and the women more horrible than the men. Besides the usual deformities in extreme old age, they acquired an additional ghastliness in proportion to their number of years, which is not to be described.

From what I had heard and seen, my keen appetite for perpetuity of life was much abated. I grew heartily ashamed of the pleasing visions I had formed, and thought no tyrant could invent a death into which I would not run with pleasure from such a life.

CHAPTER EIGHT

GULLIVER RETURNS TO ENGLAND

His Majesty having often pressed me to accept some employment in his Court, and finding me absolutely determined to return to my native country, was pleased to give me his licence to depart, and honoured me with a letter of recommendation under his own hand to the Emperor of Japan. He likewise presented me with four hundred and forty-four large pieces of gold (this nation delighting in even numbers) and a red diamond which I sold in England for eleven hundred pounds. On the sixth day of May, 1709, I took a solemn leave of His Majesty, and all my friends. I found a vessel ready to carry me to Japan, and spent fifteen days in the voyage.

We landed at a small port-town called Xamoschi, situated on the south-east part of Japan; the town lies on the western point where there is a narrow strait, leading northward into a long arm of the sea, upon the north-west part of which Yedo, the metropolis, stands. At landing, I showed the custom-house officers my letter from the King of Luggnagg to his Imperial Majesty. The magistrates of the town, hearing of my letter, received me as a public minister; they provided me with carriage and servants, and bore my charges to Yedo, where I was admitted to an audience, and delivered my letter, which was opened with great ceremony, and explained to the Emperor by an interpreter. This interpreter was a person employed to transact affairs with the Hollanders; he soon conjectured by my countenance that I was an European; and therefore repeated his Majesty's commands in Low Dutch.

On the 9th day of June, 1709, I arrived at Nangasac, after a very long and troublesome journey. I soon fell into company of some Dutch sailors. I had lived long in Holland, pursuing my studies at Leyden, and I spoke Dutch well. Nothing happened worth mentioning in this voyage. We sailed with a fair wind to the Cape of Good Hope, where we stayed only to take in fresh water. On the 16th of April we arrived safe at Amsterdam. From Amsterdam I soon after set sail for England in a small vessel belonging to the city.

On the 20th of April, 1710, we put in at the Downs. I landed next morning, and saw once more my native country after an absence of five years and six months complete. I went straight to Redriff, where I arrived the same day, and found my wife and family in good health.

PART IV: A VOYAGE TO THE COUNTRY OF THE HOUYHNHNMS

CHAPTER ONE: GULLIVER ARRIVES IN THE LAND OF THE YAHOOS AND HOUYHNHNMS

I continued at home with my wife and children about five months in a very happy condition. I left my poor wife big with child, and accepted an advantageous offer made me to be Captain of the *Adventure*, for I understood navigation well, and being grown weary of a surgeon's employment at sea, I took a skilful young man of that calling into my ship. We set sail from Portsmouth upon the seventh day of September, 1710.

I had several men die in my ship of calentures, so that I was forced to get recruits out of Barbadoes. These rogues formed a conspiracy to seize the ship and secure me; which they did one morning, rushing into my cabin, and binding me hand and foot, threatening to throw me overboard, if I offered to stir. They forced me into the long-boat, letting me put on my best suit of clothes, which were as good as new, and a small bundle of linen, but no arms except my hanger; and they were so civil as not to search my pockets, into which I conveyed what money I had, with some other little necessaries. They rowed about a league, and then set me down on a strand.

In this desolate condition I advanced forward, and soon got upon firm ground, where I sat down on a bank to rest myself, and consider what I had best to do. When I was a little refreshed, I went up into the country, resolving to deliver myself to the first savages I should meet. I walked very circumspectly for fear of being surprised, or suddenly shot with an arrow from behind or on either side. I fell into a beaten road, where I saw many tracks of human feet, and some of cows, but most of horses. At last I beheld several animals in a field, and one or two of the same kind sitting in trees. Their shape was very singular, and deformed, which a little discomposed me, so that I lay down behind a thicket to observe them better. Their heads and breasts were covered with a thick hair, some frizzled and others lank; they had beards like goats, and a long ridge of hair down their backs. They climbed high trees, as nimbly as a squirrel, for they had strong extended claws before and behind, terminating in sharp points, and hooked. They would often spring, and bound, and leap with prodigious agility. Upon the whole, I never beheld in all my travels so disagreeable an animal, nor one against which I naturally conceived so strong an antipathy.

One of these creatures coming up directly to me, lifted up his fore-paw, whether out of curiosity or mischief I could not tell. I drew my hanger, and gave him a good blow with it. The beast roared so loud that a herd of at least forty came flocking about me. I ran to the body of a tree, and, leaning my back against it, kept them off by waving my hanger. Several of this cursed brood getting hold of the branches behind leaped up onto the tree, from whence they began to discharge their excrements on my head: however, I escaped pretty well, by sticking close to the stem of the tree, but was almost stifled with the filth, which fell about me on every side.

In the midst of this distress, I observed them all to run away on a sudden as fast as they could, at which I ventured to leave the tree, and pursue the road, wondering what it was that could put them into this fright. But looking on my left hand, I saw a horse walking softly in the field, which my persecutors having sooner discovered, was the cause of their flight. The horse started a little when he came near me, but soon recovering himself, looked full in my face with manifest tokens of wonder.

We stood gazing at each other for some time. While he and I were thus employed, another horse came up; who, applying himself to the first in a very formal manner, they gently struck each other's right hoof before, neighing several times by turns, and varying the sound, which seemed to be almost articulate. They went some paces off, as if it were to confer together, walking side by side, backward and forward, like persons deliberating upon some affair of weight, but often turning their eyes towards me, as it were to watch that I might not escape. I was amazed to see such actions and behaviour in brute beasts, and concluded with myself, that if the inhabitants of this country were endued with a proportionable degree of reason, they must needs be the wisest people upon earth.

Upon the whole, the behaviour of these animals was so orderly and rational, so acute and judicious, that I at last concluded, they must needs be magicians, who had thus metamorphosed themselves upon some design, and seeing a stranger in the way, were resolved to divert themselves with him; or perhaps were really amazed at the sight of a man so very different in habit, feature, and complexion from those who might probably live in so remote a climate. Upon the strength of this reasoning, I ventured to address them in the following manner: Gentleman, if you be conjurers, as I have good cause to believe, you can understand any language; therefore I make bold to let your Worships know, that I am a poor distressed Englishman, driven by his misfortunes upon your coast, and I entreat one of you, to let me ride upon his back, as if he were a real horse, to some house or village, where I can be relieved. The two creatures stood silent while I spoke, seeming to listen with great attention; and when I had ended, they neighed frequently towards each other, as if they were engaged in serious conversation. I plainly observed that their language expressed the passions very well, and the words might with little pains be resolved into an alphabet more easily than the Chinese.

I could frequently distinguish the word *Yahoo*, which was repeated by each of them several times; and although it were impossible for me to conjecture what it meant, yet while the two horses were busy in conversation, I endeavoured to practise this word upon my tongue; and as soon as they were silent, I boldly pronounced *Yahoo* in a loud voice, imitating, at the same time, as near as I could, the neighing of a horse; at which they were both visibly surprised, and the gray repeated the same word twice, as if he meant to teach me the right accent, wherein I spoke after him as well as I could, and found myself perceivably to improve every time, although very far from any degree of perfection. Then the bay tried to teach me with a second word, much harder to be pronounced; but reducing it to the English orthography, may be spelt thus, *Houyhnhnm*. I did not succeed in this so well as the former, but after two or three farther trials, I had better fortune; and they both appeared amazed at my capacity. After some further discourse, which I conjectured might relate to me, the two friends took their leaves, and the first horse, who was a dapple-gray, made me signs that I should walk before him.

CHAPTER TWO

GULLIVER SAVES HIMSELF FROM STARVATION

Having travelled about three miles, we came to a long kind of building, made of timber stuck in the ground, and wattled across; the roof was low, and covered with straw. I now began to be a little comforted, and took out some toys, which travellers usually carry for presents to the savage Indians of America and other parts, in hopes the people of the house would be thereby encouraged to receive me kindly. The horse made me a sign to go in first; it was a large room with a smooth clay floor, and a rack and manger extending the whole length on one side. There were horses inside. The gray came in just after, and thereby prevented any ill treatment, which the others might have given me. He neighed to them several times in a style of authority, and received answers.

Beyond this room there were others, reaching the length of the house; we went through the second room toward the third; here the gray walked in first, beckoning me to attend; I waited in the second room. The horse neighed three or four times, and I waited to hear some answers in a human voice, but I heard no other returns than in the same dialect. I feared my brain was disturbed by my sufferings and misfortunes: I roused myself, and looked about me in the room where I was left alone; this was furnished as the first, only after a more elegant manner. The gray horse came to the door, and made me a sign to follow him into the third room, where I saw a very comely mare, together with a colt and foal, sitting on their haunches, upon mats of straw, not unartfully made, and perfectly neat and clean.

The mare, soon after my entrance, rose from her mat, and coming up close, after having nicely observed my hands and face, gave me a most contemptuous look; then turning to the horse, I heard the word *Yahoo* often repeated betwixt them; the meaning of which word I could not then comprehend. I saw three of those detestable creatures, which I first met after my landing, feeding upon roots, and the flesh of some animals, which I afterwards found to be that of asses and dogs, and now and then a cow dead by accident or disease. They were all tied by the neck with strong withes, fastened to a beam; they held their food between the claws of their fore-feet, and tore it with their teeth.

The master horse ordered a sorrel nag, one of his servants, to untie the largest of these animals, and take him into the yard. The beast and I were brought close together, and our countenances diligently compared, both by master and servant, who thereupon repeated several times the word *Yahoo*. My horror and astonishment are not to be described, when I observed, in this abominable animal, a perfect human figure.

The great difficulty that seemed to stick with the two horses, was to see the rest of my body so very different from that of a Yahoo, for which I was obliged to my clothes, whereof they had no conception: the sorrel nag offered me a root. I took it in my hand, and having smelt it, returned it to him as civilly as I could. He brought out of the Yahoo's kennel a piece of ass's flesh, but it smelt so offensively that I turned from it with loathing; he then threw it to the Yahoo, by whom it was greedily devoured. He afterwards showed me a wisp of hay and a fetlock full of oats; but I shook my head, to signify that neither of these were food for me. And indeed, I now apprehended that I must absolutely starve, if I did not get to some of my own species; for as to those filthy Yahoos, I confess I never saw any sensitive being so detestable on all accounts; and the more I came near them, the more hateful they grew, while I stayed in that country. This the master horse observed by my behaviour, and therefore sent the Yahoo back to his kennel. While we were thus engaged, I observed a cow passing by, whereupon I pointed to her, and expressed a desire to let me go and milk her. This had its effect; for he led me back into the house, and ordered a mare-servant to open a room, where a good store of milk lay in earthen and wooden vessels, after a very orderly and cleanly manner. She gave me a large bowl full, of which I drank very heartily, and found myself well refreshed.

When dinner was done, the master horse took me aside, and by signs and words made me understand the concern he was in, that I had nothing to eat. I considered that I could contrive to make of oats a kind of bread, which might be sufficient with milk to keep me alive, till I could make my escape to some other country, and to creatures of my own species. The horse immediately ordered a white mare-servant of his family to bring me a good quantity of oats in a sort of wooden tray. These I heated before the fire as well as I could, and rubbed them till the husks came off, which I made a shift to winnow from the grain; I ground and beat them between two stones, then took water, and made them into a paste or cake, which I toasted at the fire, and ate warm with milk. It was at first a very insipid diet, although common enough in many parts of Europe, but grew tolerable by time; and having been often reduced to hard fare in my life, this was not the first experiment I had made to prove how easily nature is satisfied. Tis true, I sometimes made a shift to catch a rabbit, or bird, by springs made of Yahoos' hairs, and I often gathered wholesome herbs, which I boiled, or ate as salads with my bread.

When it grew towards evening, the master horse ordered a place for me to lodge in; it was but six yards from the house, and separated from the stable of the Yahoos. Here I got some straw, and covering myself with my own clothes, slept very sound. But I was in a short time better accommodated.

CHAPTER THREE

GULLIVER LEARNS THE LANGUAGE OF THE HOUYHNHNMS

My principal endeavour was to learn the language, which my master (for so I shall henceforth call him) and his children, and every servant of his house were desirous to teach me. For they looked upon it as a prodigy that a brute animal should discover such marks of a rational creature. I pointed to everything, and enquired the name of it, which I wrote down in my journal-book when I was alone, and corrected my bad accent, by desiring those of the family to pronounce it often. In this employment, a sorrel nag, one of the under servants, was very ready to assist me.

In about ten weeks' time I was able to understand most of my master's questions, and in three months could give him some tolerable answers. He was extremely curious to know from what part of the country I came, and how I was taught to imitate a rational creature. I answered, that I came over the sea, from a far place, with many others of my own kind, in a great hollow vessel made of the bodies of trees. He replied, that I must needs be mistaken, or that I *said the thing which was not.* (For they have no word in their language to express lying or falsehood.) He knew it was impossible that there could be a country beyond the sea, or that a parcel of brutes could move a wooden vessel whither they pleased upon water. He was sure no Houyhnhnm alive could make such a vessel, nor would trust Yahoos to manage it.

He was pleased to direct his own mare, his colt and foal, and the servants of the family to take all opportunities of instructing me, and every day for two or three hours, he was at the same pains himself. I made so great a progress, that in five months from my arrival, I understood whatever was spoke, and could express myself tolerably well.

The Houyhnhnms who came to visit my master, out of a design of seeing and talking with me, could hardly believe me to be a right Yahoo, because my body had a different covering from others of my kind. They were astonished to observe me without the usual hair or skin, except on my head, face, and hands.

I had hitherto concealed the secret of my dress, in order to distinguish myself as much as possible, from that cursed race of Yahoos; but now I found it in vain to do so any longer. Besides, I considered that my clothes and shoes would soon wear out, which already were in a declining condition. I therefore told my master, that in the country from whence I came, those of my kind always covered their bodies to avoid inclemencies of air both hot and cold; of which, I would give him immediate conviction, if he pleased to command me; only desiring his excuse, if I did not expose those parts that Nature taught us to conceal. He said my discourse was all very strange, but especially the last part; for he could not understand why Nature should teach us to conceal what Nature had given. That neither himself nor family were ashamed of any parts of their bodies.

I expressed my uneasiness at his giving me so often the appellation of *Yahoo*, an odious animal, for which I had so utter an hatred and contempt; I begged he would forbear applying that word to me, and take the same order in his family, and among his friends whom he suffered to see me. I requested likewise, that the secret of my having a false covering to my body might be known to none but himself, at least as long as my present clothing should last.

In the meantime, he desired I would go on with my utmost diligence to learn their language, because he was more astonished at my capacity for speech and reason, than at the figure of my body, whether it were covered or no; adding, that he waited with some impatience to hear the wonders which I promised to tell him.

Every day when I waited on him, he would ask me several questions concerning myself, which I answered as well as I could. I said:

That, I came from a very far country, with about fifty more of my own species; that we travelled upon the seas, in a great hollow vessel made of wood. He asked me, who made the ship, and how it was possible that the Houyhnhnm of my country would leave it to the management of brutes? I went on by assuring him that the ship was made by creatures like myself, who in all the countries I had travelled, as well as in my own, were the only governing, rational animals; and that upon my arrival hither, I was as much astonished to see the Houyhnhnms act like rational beings, as he or his friends could be in finding some marks of reason in a creature he was pleased to call a Yahoo, to which I owned my resemblance in every part, but could not account for their degenerate and brutal nature.

When I asserted that the Yahoos were the only governing animals in my country, which my master said was altogether past his conception, he desired to know, whether we had Houyhnhnms among us, and what was their employment: I told him, we had great numbers, that in summer they grazed in the fields, and in winter were kept in houses, with hay and oats, where Yahoo servants were employed to rub their skins smooth, comb their manes, pick their feet, serve them with food, and make their beds. I understand you well, said my master; it is now very plain, from all you have spoken, that whatever share of reason the Yahoos pretend to, the Houyhnhnms are your masters; I heartily wish our Yahoos would be so tractable. I begged His Honour would please to excuse me from proceeding any farther, because I was very certain that the account he expected from me would be highly displeasing. But he insisted in commanding me to let him know the best and the worst.

I owned, that the Houyhnhnms among us, whom we called *horses*, were the most generous and comely animal we had, that they excelled in strength and swiftness; and when they belonged to persons of quality, employed in travelling, racing, or drawing chariots, they were treated with much kindness and care, till they fell into diseases, or became foundered in the feet; but then they were sold, and used to all kind of drudgery till they died; after which their skins were stripped and sold for what they were worth, and their bodies left to be devoured by dogs and birds of prey. But the common race of horses had not so good fortune, being kept by farmers and carriers and other mean people, who put them to greater labour, and fed them worse.

My master, after some expressions of great indignation, wondered how we dared to venture upon a Houyhnhnm's back, for he was sure that the weakest servant in his house would be able to shake off the strongest Yahoo, or by lying down, and rolling upon his back, squeeze the brute to death. I answered, that our horses were trained up from three or four years old to the several uses we intended them for; that if any of them proved intolerably vicious, they were employed for carriages; that they were severely beaten while they were young, for any mischievous tricks; that the males, designed for the common use of riding or draught, were generally *castrated* about two years after their birth, to take down their spirits, and make them more tame and gentle; that they were indeed sensible of rewards and punishments; but His Honour would please to consider, that they had not the least tincture of reason any more than the Yahoos in this country.

It is impossible to express his noble resentment at our savage treatment of the Houyhnhnm race, particularly after I had explained the manner and use of *castrating* horses among us, to hinder them from propagating their kind, and to render them more servile. However, he would (as he said) debate that matter no farther, because he was more desirous to know my own story, the country where I was born, and the several actions and events of my life before I came hither.

I said, my birth was of honest parents, in an island called England, that I was bred a surgeon, whose trade it is to cure wounds and hurts in the body, got by accident or violence; that my country was governed by a female man, whom we called a *Queen*. That I left it to get riches, whereby I might maintain myself and family when I should return. Here my master interposed, by asking me, how I could persuade strangers out of different countries to venture with me, after the losses I had sustained, and the hazards I had run. I said, they were fellows of desperate fortunes; forced to fly from the places of their crimes. Some were undone by lawsuits; others spent all they had in drinking, whoring and gaming; others fled for treason; many for murder, theft, poisoning, robbery, perjury, forgery, coining false money, for committing rapes or sodomy, for flying from their colours, or deserting to the enemy, and most of them had broken prison; none of these durst return to their native countries for fear of being hanged, or of starving in a jail; and therefore were under a necessity of seeking a livelihood in other places.

My master was wholly at a loss to know what could be the use or necessity of practising those vices. To clear up which I endeavoured to give him some ideas of the desire of power and riches, of the terrible effects of lust, intemperance, malice and envy. Like one whose imagination was struck with something never seen or heard of before, he would lift up his eyes with amazement and indignation. Power, government, war, law, punishment, and a thousand other things had no terms, wherein that language could express them, which made the difficulty almost insuperable to give my master any conception of what I meant. But being of an excellent understanding, much improved by contemplation and converse, he at last arrived at a competent knowledge of what human nature in our parts of the world is capable to perform, and desired I would give him some particular account of that land, which we call Europe, but especially, of my own country.

CHAPTER FOUR

ON WARS AND LAW

In obedience to His Honour's commands, I related to him the Revolution under the Prince of Orange, the long war with France entered into by the said Prince, and renewed by his successor the present Queen. I computed, at his request, that about a million of Yahoos might have been killed in the whole progress of it, and perhaps a hundred or more cities taken, and five times as many ships burnt or sunk.

He asked me what were the usual causes or motives that made one country go to war with another. I answered they were innumerable, but I should only mention a few of the chief. Sometimes the ambition of princes, who never think they have land or people enough to govern: sometimes the corruption of ministers, who engage their master in a war in order to stifle or divert the clamour of the subjects against their evil administration. Difference in opinions hath cost many millions of lives: for instance, whether *flesh* be *bread*, or *bread* be *flesh*; whether the juice of a certain *berry* be *blood* or *wine*; with many more.

Sometimes the quarrel between two princes is to decide which of them shall dispossess a third of his dominions, where neither of them pretend to any right. Alliance by blood or marriage is a sufficient cause of war between princes, and the nearer the kindred is, the greater is their disposition to quarrel: *poor* nations are *hungry*, and *rich* nations are *proud*, and pride and hunger will ever be at variance. For these reasons, the trade of a *soldier* is held the most honourable of all others: because a *soldier* is a Yahoo hired to kill in cold blood as many of his own species, who have never offended him, as possibly he can.

There was another point which a little perplexed him at present. I had said, that some of our crew left their country on account of being ruined by *law*; that I had already explained the meaning of the word; but he was at a loss how it should come to pass, that the *law* which was intended for *every* man's preservation, should be any man's ruin. He thought Nature and Reason were sufficient guides for a reasonable animal, as we pretended to be, in showing us what we ought to do, and what to avoid.

I said there was a society of men among us, bred up, from their youth, in the art of proving by words multiplied for the purpose, that white is black and black is white, according as they are paid. To this society all the rest of the people are slaves. For example, if my neighbour hath a mind to my cow, he hires a lawyer to prove that he ought to have my cow from me. I must then hire another to defend my right, it being against all rules of law that any man should be allowed to speak for himself. Now in this case, I who am the true owner lie under two great disadvantages. First, my lawyer, being practised almost from his cradle in defending falsehood, is quite out of his element when he would be an advocate for justice. The second disadvantage is, that my lawyer must proceed with great caution, or else he will be reprimanded by the Judges, and abhorred by his brethren, as one who would lessen the practice of the law. And therefore I have but two methods to preserve my cow. The first is to gain over my adversary's lawyer with a double fee, who will then betray his client by insinuating that he hath justice on his side. The second way is for my lawyer to make my cause appear as unjust as he can, by allowing the cow to belong to my adversary; and this if it be skilfully done will certainly bespeak the favour of the Bench.

Now, Your Honour is to know that these Judges are persons appointed to decide all controversies of property, as well as for the trial of criminals, and picked out from the most dexterous lawyers who are grown old or lazy, and having been biased all their lives against truth and equity, lie under such a fatal necessity of favouring fraud, perjury, and oppression, that I have known several of them refuse a large bribe from the side where justice lay, rather than injure the *Faculty* by doing anything unbecoming their nature or their office.

In the trial of persons accused for crimes against the state the method is much more short and commendable: the Judge first sends to sound the disposition of those in power, after which he can easily hang or save the criminal, strictly preserving all the forms of law.

My master was yet wholly at a loss to understand what motives could incite this race of lawyers to perplex, disquiet, and weary themselves by engaging in a confederacy of injustice, merely for the sake of injuring their fellow-animals; neither could he comprehend what I meant in saying they did it for *hire.* Whereupon I was at much pains to describe to him the use of *money*, the materials it was made of, and the value of the metals; that when a Yahoo had got a great store of this precious substance, he was able to purchase whatever he had a mind to. Therefore since *money* alone was able to perform all these feats, our Yahoos thought they could never have enough of it to spend or to save as they found themselves inclined from their natural bent either to profusion or avarice. That the rich man enjoyed the fruit of the poor man's labour, and the latter were a thousand to one in proportion to the former. That the bulk of our people was forced to live miserably, by labouring every day for small wages to make a few live plentifully. In order to feed the luxury and intemperance of the males, and the vanity of the females, we sent away the greatest part of our necessary things to other countries, from whence in return we brought the materials of diseases, folly, and vice, to spend among ourselves. Hence it follows of necessity, that vast numbers of our people are compelled to seek their livelihood by begging, robbing, stealing, cheating, pimping, forswearing, flattering, suborning, forging, gaming, lying, fawning, hectoring, voting, scribbling, stargazing, poisoning, whoring, canting, libelling, free-thinking, and the like occupations: every one of which terms, I was at much pains to make him understand.

CHAPTER FIVE

THE YAHOOS

I must freely confess, that the many virtues of those excellent *quadrupeds*, placed in opposite view to human corruptions, had so far opened mine eyes and enlarged my understanding, that I began to view the actions and passions of man in a very different light; besides, it was impossible for me to do before a person of so acute a judgement as my master, who daily convinced me of a thousand faults in myself, whereof I had not the least perception before. I had likewise learned from his example an utter detestation of all falsehood or disguise; and *truth* appeared so amiable to me, that I determined upon sacrificing everything to it.

I had not been a year in this country before I contracted such a love and veneration for the inhabitants, that I entered on a firm resolution never to return to humankind, but to pass the rest of my life among these admirable Houyhnhnms in the contemplation and practice of every virtue; where I could have no example or incitement to vice. But it was decreed by Fortune, my perpetual enemy, that so great a felicity should not fall to my share. However, it is now some comfort to reflect, that in what I said of my countrymen, I *extenuated* their faults as much as I durst before so strict an examiner, and upon every article gave as *favourable* a turn as the matter would bear. For, indeed, who is there alive that will not be swayed by his bias and partiality to the place of his birth?

When I had answered all his questions, and his curiosity seemed to be fully satisfied, he sent for me one morning early, and commanding me to sit down at some distance (an honour which he had never before conferred upon me), he said, he had been very seriously considering my whole story, as far as it related both to myself and my country: that he looked upon us as a sort of animals to whose share, by what accident he could not conjecture, some small pittance of *Reason* had fallen, whereof we made no other use than by its assistance to aggravate our *natural* corruptions, and to acquire new ones which Nature had not given us.

He said the Yahoos were known to hate one another more than they did any different species of animals; and the reason usually assigned, was, the odiousness of their own shapes, which all could see in the rest, but not in themselves. He had therefore begun to think it not unwise in us to *cover* our bodies, and, by that invention, conceal many of our deformities from each other, which would else be hardly supportable. But, he now found he had been mistaken, and that the dissensions of those brutes in his country were owing to the same cause with ours, as I had described them. For if (said he) you throw among five Yahoos as much food as would be sufficient for fifty, they will, instead of eating peaceably, fall together by the ears, each single one impatient to *have all to itself*; and therefore a servant was usually employed to stand by while they were feeding abroad, and those kept at home were tied at a distance from each other; that if a cow died of age or accident, before a Houyhnhnm could secure it for his own Yahoos, those in the neighbourhood would come in herds to seize it, and then would ensue such a battle as I had described, with terrible wounds made by their claws on both sides, although they seldom were able to kill one another, for want of such convenient instruments of death as we had invented. At other times the like battles have been fought between the Yahoos of several neighbourhoods without any visible cause: those of one district watching all opportunities to surprise the next before they are prepared. But if they find their project hath miscarried, they return home, and for want of enemies, engage in what I call a *civil war* among themselves.

I did indeed observe, that the Yahoos were the only animals in this country subject to any diseases and the cure prescribed is a mixture of *their own dung and urine* forcibly put down the Yahoo's throat. This I have since often known to have been taken with success, and do here freely recommend it to my countrymen, for the public good, as an admirable specific against all diseases produced by repletion.

He had heard that in most herds there was a sort of ruling Yahoo who was always more *deformed* in body, and *mischievous in disposition*, than any of the rest. That this *leader* had usually a favourite as *like himself* as he could get, whose employment was to *lick his master's feet and posteriors, and drive the female Yahoos to his kennel*; for which he was now and then rewarded with a piece of ass's flesh. This favourite is hated by the whole herd, and therefore to protect himself, keeps always *near the person of his leader*. He usually continues in office till a worse can be found; but the very moment he is discarded, his successor, at the head of all the Yahoos in that district, young and old, male and female, come in a body, and discharge their excrements upon him from head to foot.

I often begged His Honour to let me go among the herds of Yahoos in the neighbourhood, to which he always very graciously consented, being perfectly convinced that the hatred I bore these brutes would never suffer me to be corrupted by them; and His Honour ordered one of his servants, a strong sorrel nag, very honest and good-natured, to be my guard, without whose protection I durst not undertake such adventures.

Being one day abroad with my protector the sorrel nag, and the weather exceeding hot, I entreated him to let me bathe in a river that was near. He consented, and I immediately stripped myself stark naked, and went down softly into the stream. It happened that a young female Yahoo, standing behind a bank, saw the whole proceeding, and inflamed by desire, as the nag and I conjectured, came running with all speed, and leaped into the water within five yards of the place where I bathed. I was never in my life so terribly frighted; the nag was grazing at some distance, not suspecting any harm. She embraced me after a most fulsome manner; I roared as loud as I could, and the nag came galloping towards me, whereupon she quitted her grasp, with the utmost reluctancy, and leaped upon the opposite bank, where she stood gazing and howling all the time I was putting on my clothes.

This was matter of diversion to my master and his family, as well as of mortification to myself. For now I could no longer deny, that I was a real Yahoo in every limb and feature, since the females had a natural propensity to me as one of their own species.

As these noble Houyhnhnms are endowed by Nature with a general disposition to all virtues, and have no conceptions or ideas of what is evil in a rational creature, so their grand maxim is to cultivate Reason and to be wholly governed by it. So that controversies, wranglings, disputes and positiveness in false or dubious propositions are evils unknown among the Houyhnhnms. In the like manner, when I used to explain to him our several systems of *natural philosophy*, he would laugh that a creature pretending to *Reason* should value itself upon the knowledge of other people's conjectures.

Friendship and benevolence are the two principal virtues among the Houyhnhnms, and these not confined to particular objects, but universal to the whole race. For a stranger from the remotest part is equally treated with the nearest neighbour, and wherever he goes, looks upon himself as at home. They preserve *decency* and *civility* in the highest degrees, but are altogether ignorant of *ceremony*. They have no fondness for their colts or foals, but the care they take in educating them proceedeth entirely from the dictates of *Reason*. And I observed my master to show the same affection to his neighbour's issue that he had for his own. They will have it that *Nature* teaches them to love the whole species, and it is *Reason* only that maketh a distinction of persons, where there is a superior degree of virtue.

Temperance, industry, exercise and *cleanliness*, are the lessons equally enjoined to the young ones of both sexes: and my master thought it monstrous in us to give the females a different kind of education from the males, except in some articles of domestic management; whereby as he truly observed, one half of our natives were good for nothing but bringing children into the world: and to trust the care of their children to such useless animals, he said, was yet a greater instance of brutality.

The Houyhnhnms train up their youth to strength, speed and hardiness, by exercising them in running races up and down steep hills, or over hard stony grounds, and when they are all in a sweat, they are ordered to leap over head and ears into a pond or a river. Four times a year the youth of certain districts meet to show their proficiency in running, and leaping, and other feats of strength or agility, where the victor is rewarded with a song made in his or her praise.

Every fourth year, at the *vernal equinox*, there is a Representative Council of the whole nation, which meets in a plain about twenty miles from our house, and continueth about five or six days. Here they enquire into the state and condition of the several districts. And wherever there is any want it is immediately supplied by unanimous consent and contribution.

CHAPTER SIX

THE GENERAL ASSEMBLY OF THE HOUYHNHNMS

One of these grand Assemblies was held in my time, about three months before my departure, whither my master went as the Representive of our district. In this Council was resumed their old debate.

The question to be debated was, whether the Yahoos should be exterminated from the face of the earth. One of the members for the affirmative offered several arguments of great strength and weight, alleging, that as the Yahoos were the most filthy, noisome, and deformed animal which Nature ever produced, so they were the most restive and indocible, mischievous and malicious: they would privately suck the teats of the Houyhnhnms' cows, kill and devour their cats, trample down their oats and grass, if they were not continually watched. He took notice of a general tradition, that Yahoos had not been always in their country: but, that many ages ago, two of these brutes appeared together upon a mountain, whether produced by the heat of the sun upon corrupted mud and slime, or from the ooze and froth of the sea, was never known. That the inhabitants taking a fancy to use the service of the Yahoos, had very imprudently neglected to cultivate the breed of asses, which were a comely animal, easily kept, more tame and orderly, without any offensive smell, strong enough for labour, although they yield to the other in agility of body; and if their braying be no agreeable sound, it is far preferable to the horrible howlings of the Yahoos.

This was all my master thought fit to tell me at that time, of what passed in the Grand Council. But he was pleased to conceal one particular, which related personally to myself, whereof I soon felt the unhappy effect, as the reader will know in its proper place, and from whence I date all the succeeding misfortunes of my life.

The Houyhnhnms have not letters, and consequently their knowledge is all traditional. I have already observed, that they are subject to no diseases, and therefore can have no need of physicians. However, they have excellent medicines composed of herbs, to cure accidental bruises and cuts.

In poetry they must be allowed to excel all other mortals, wherein the justness of their similes, and the minuteness, as well as exactness of their descriptions, are indeed inimitable. Their verses abound very much in both of these, and usually contain either some exalted notions of friendship and benevolence, or the praises of those who were victors in races, and other bodily exercises.

The Houyhnhnms use the hollow part between the pastern and the hoof of their fore-feet as we do our hands, and this with greater dexterity than I could at first imagine. They milk their cows, reap their oats, and do all the work which requires hands, in the same manner. They have a kind of hard flints, which by grinding against other stones, they form into instruments, that serve instead of wedges, axes, and hammers. With tools made of these flints they likewise cut their hay, and reap their oats, the Yahoos draw home the sheaves in carriages, and the servants tread them in certain covered huts, to get out the grain, which is kept in stores. They make a rude kind of earthen and wooden vessels, and bake the former in the sun.

If they can avoid casualties, they die only of old age, and are buried in the obscurest places that can be found, their friends and relations expressing neither joy nor grief at their departure; nor does the dying person discover the least regret that he is leaving the world, any more than if he were upon returning home from a visit to one of his neighbours.

CHAPTER SEVEN

GULLIVER PREPARES TO LEAVE THE LAND

I had settled my little economy to my own heart's content. My master had ordered a room to be made for me after their manner, about six yards from the house. I had worked two chairs with my knife, the sorrel nag helping me in the grosser and more laborious part. When my clothes were worn to rags, I made myself others with the skins of rabbits, I often got honey out of hollow trees, which I mingled with water, or ate it with my bread. No man could more verify the truth of these two maxims, *that nature is very easily satisfied*; and, *that necessity is the mother of invention.* I enjoyed perfect health of body and tranquillity of mind; I did not feel the treachery or inconstancy of a friend, nor the injuries of a secret or open enemy. I had no occasion of bribing, flattering or pimping, to procure the favour of any great man or of his minion. I wanted no fence against fraud or oppression; here was neither physician to destroy my body, nor lawyer to ruin my fortune; no informer to watch my words and actions, or force accusations against me for hire.

I had the favour of being admitted to several Houyhnhnms, who came to visit or dine with my master; where His Honour graciously suffered me to wait in the room, and listen to their discourse. Both he and his company would often descend to ask me questions, and receive my answers. I had also sometimes the honour of attending my master in his visits to others. I never presumed to speak, except in answer to a question, and then I did it with inward regret, because it was a loss of so much time for improving myself: but I was infinitely delighted with the station of an humble auditor in such conversations, where nothing passed but what was useful, expressed in the fewest and most significant words.

I freely confess, that all the little knowledge I have of any value, was acquired by the lectures I received from my master, and from hearing the discourses of him and his friends. I admired the strength, comeliness, and speed of the inhabitants; and such a constellation of virtues in such amiable persons produced in me the highest veneration.

When I happened to behold the reflection of my own form in a lake or a fountain, I turned away my face in horror and detestation of myself, and could better endure the sight of a common Yahoo, than of my own person. By conversing with the Houyhnhnms, and looking upon them with delight, I fell to imitate their gait and gesture, which is now grown into a habit, and my friends often tell me in a blunt way, that *I trot like a horse*; which, however, I take for a great compliment: neither shall I disown, that in speaking I am apt to fall into the voice and manner of the Houyhnhnms, and hear myself ridiculed on that account without the least mortification.

In the midst of all this happiness, when I looked upon myself to be fully settled for life, my master sent for me one morning a little earlier than his usual hour. I observed by his countenance that he was in some perplexity. He told me that in the last General Assembly, the Representatives had taken offence at his keeping a Yahoo (meaning myself) in his family more like a Houyhnhnm, than a brute animal. The Assembly did therefore *exhort* him, either to employ me like the rest of my species, or command me to swim back to the place from whence I came.

I was struck with the utmost grief and despair at my master's discourse, and being unable to support the agonies I was under, I fell into a swoon at his feet; when I came to myself, he told me, that he concluded I had been dead. I answered, in a faint voice, that death would have been too great an happiness; that the certain prospect of an unnatural death was the least of my evils: for, supposing I should escape with life by some strange adventure, how could I think with temper of passing my days among Yahoos, and relapsing into my old corruptions, for want of examples to lead and keep me within the paths of virtue?

My master in a few words made me a very gracious reply, allowed me the space of two months to finish my boat; and ordered the sorrel nag, my fellow-servant, to follow my instructions.

I returned home, and consulting with the sorrel nag, we went into a copse at some distance, where I with my knife, and he with a sharp flint fastened very artificially, after their manner, to a wooden handle, cut down several oak wattles about the thickness of a walking-staff, and some larger pieces. In six weeks' time, with the help of the sorrel nag, who performed the parts that required most labour, I finished a sort of Indian canoe, but much larger, covering it with the skins of Yahoos well stitched together, with hempen threads of my own making. I laid in a stock of boiled flesh, of rabbits and fowls, and took with me two vessels; one filled with milk, and the other with water.

When all was ready, and the day came for my departure, I took leave of my master and lady, and the whole family, mine eyes flowing with tears, and my heart quite sunk with grief. As I was going to prostrate myself to kiss his hoof, he did me the honour to raise it gently to my mouth. I paid my respects to the rest of the Houyhnhnms in His Honour's company; then getting into my canoe, I pushed off from shore.

CHAPTER EIGHT

GULLIVER ARRIVES HOME

I began this desperate voyage on February 15, 1715. The wind was very favourable. My master and his friends continued on the shore, till I was almost out of sight; and I often heard the sorrel nag: take care of thyself, gentle Yahoo.

My design was, if possible, to discover some small island uninhabited, yet sufficient by my labour to furnish me with the necessaries of life. For in such a solitude as I desired, I could at least enjoy my own thoughts, and reflect with delight on the virtues of those inimitable Houyhnhnms, without any opportunity of degenerating into the vices and corruptions of my own species.

I resolved to steer my course eastward, hoping to reach the south-west coast of New Holland. By six in the evening I computed I had gone eastward at least eighteen leagues, when I spied a very small island about half a league off, which I soon reached. It was nothing but a rock with one creek. Here I put in my canoe, and climbing a part of the rock, I could plainly discover land to the east, extending from south to north. I lay all night in my canoe, and repeating my voyage early in the morning, I arrived in seven hours to the south-west point of New Holland.

On the fourth day, venturing out early a little too far, I saw twenty or thirty natives upon a height, not above five hundred yards from me. They were stark naked, men, women, and children, round a fire, as I could discover by the smoke. One of them spied me, and gave notice to the rest; five of them advanced towards me, leaving the women and children at the fire. I made what haste I could to the shore, and getting into my canoe, shoved off: the savages observing me retreat, ran after me; and before I could get far enough into the sea, discharged an arrow, which wounded me deeply on the inside of my left knee.

As I was looking about for a secure landing-place, I saw a sail to the north-north-east, and turning my canoe, I sailed and paddled together to the south, and got into the same creek from whence I set out in the morning, choosing rather to trust myself among these *barbarians*, than live with European Yahoos. I drew up my canoe and hid myself behind a stone.

The ship came within half a league of this creek, and sent out her long-boat with vessels to take in fresh water. The seamen at their landing observed my canoe, and rummaging it all over, easily conjectured that the owner could not be far off. They searched every cranny and lurking-hole, till at last they found me. One of the seamen in Portuguese bid me rise, and asked who I was. I understood that language very well, and getting upon my feet, said, I was a poor Yahoo, banished from the Houyhnhnms, but they were at a loss to know what I meant by Yahoos and Houyhnhnms, and at the same time fell a laughing at my strange tone in speaking, which resembled the neighing of a horse.

When they began to talk, I thought I never heard or saw anything so unnatural; for it appeared to me as monstrous as if a dog or a cow should speak in England, or a Yahoo in Houyhnhnmland. The honest Portuguese were equally amazed at my strange dress, and the old manner of delivering my words, which however they understood very well. They spoke to me with great humanity, and said they were sure their captain would carry me *gratis* to Lisbon, from whence I might return to my own country. I was taken into the ship, and from thence into the captain's cabin.

His name was Pedro de Mendez; he was a very courteous and generous person. However, I remained silent and sullen; I was ready to faint at the very smell of him and his men. At last I desired something to eat out of my own canoe; but he ordered me a chicken and some excellent wine, and then directed that I should be put to bed in a very clean cabin.

After dinner Don Pedro came to me, and assured me he only meant to do me all the service he was able, and spoke so very movingly, that at last I descended to treat him like an animal which had some little portion of Reason.

Our voyage passed without any considerable accident. In gratitude to the captain I sometimes sat with him at his earnest request, and strove to conceal my antipathy against human kind. The Captain had often entreated me to strip myself of my savage dress, and offered to lend me the best suit of clothes he had. This I would not be prevailed on to accept, abhorring to cover myself with anything that had been on the back of a Yahoo. I only desired he would lend me two clean shirts, which having been washed since he wore them, I believed would not so much defile me.

We arrived at Lisbon, Nov. 5, 1715. I was conveyed to the captain's own house. He had no wife, nor above three servants, none of which were suffered to attend at meals, and his whole department was so obliging, added to very good human understanding, that I really began to tolerate his company. In ten days Don Pedro, to whom I had given some account of my domestic affairs, put it upon me as a point of honour and conscience, that I ought to return to my native country, and live at home with my wife and children.

I complied at last, finding I could not do better. I left Lisbon the 24th day of November, in an English merchantman, but who was the master I never inquired. Don Pedro accompanied me to the ship, and lent me twenty pounds. He took kind leave of me, and embraced me at parting, which I bore as well as I could.

My wife and family received me with great surprise and joy, because they concluded me certainly dead; but I must freely confess the sight of them filled me only with hatred, disgust and contempt, and the more by reflecting on the near alliance I had to them. For, although since my unfortunate exile from the Houyhnhnm country, I had compelled myself to tolerate the sight of Yahoos, and to converse with Don Pedro de Mendez, yet my memory and imaginations were perpetually filled with the virtues and ideas of those exalted Houyhnhnms.

As soon as I entered the house, my wife took me in her arms, and kissed me, at which having not been used to the touch of that odious animal for so many years, I fell in a swoon for almost an hour At the time I am writing, it is five years since my last return to England: during the first year I could not endure my wife or children in my presence, the very smell of them was intolerable. The first money I laid out was to buy two stone-horses which I keep in a good stable, and next to them the groom is my greatest favourite, for I feel my spirits revived by the smell he contracts in the stable. My horses understand me tolerably well; I converse with them at least four hours every day. They are strangers to bridle or saddle, they live in great amity with me, and friendship to each other.

Farewell to the Reader

I here take a final leave of my courteous readers, and return to enjoy my own speculations in my little garden at Redriff, to apply those excellent lessons of virtue which I learned among the Houyhnhnms, to instruct the Yahoos of my own family as far as I shall find them docible animals, to behold my figure often in a glass, and thus if possible habituate myself by time to tolerate the sight of a human creature.

I began last week to permit my wife to sit at dinner with me, at the farthest end of a long table. Yet the smell of a Yahoo continuing very offensive, I always keep my nose well stopped with rue, lavender, or tobacco leaves.

My reconcilement to the Yahoo-kind in general might not be so difficult if they would be content with those vices and follies only, which Nature hath entitled them to. But when I behold a lump of deformity and diseases both in body and mind, smitten with *pride*, it immediately breaks all the measure of my patience; neither shall I be ever able to comprehend how such an animal and such a vice could tally together. The wise and virtuous Houyhnhnms, who abound in all excellencies that can adorn a rational creature, have no name for this vice in their language. They live under the government of Reason and are no more proud of the good qualities they possess than I should be for not wanting a leg or an arm, which no man in his wits would boast of, although he must be miserable without them. I dwell the longer upon this subject from the desire I have to make the society of an English Yahoo by any means not insupportable, and therefore I here entreat those who have any tincture of this absurd vice, that they will not presume to appear in my sight.

SUMMARIES, GLOSSARY AND COMPREHENSION

PART I: A VOYAGE TO LILLIPUT

PART I: CHAPTER 1

SUMMARY

Gulliver was the third of five sons and went to Emmanuel College in Cambridge. He became an apprentice to Mr Bates with whom he worked for four years. However, Gulliver loved to travel. His reason for studying medicine was because it would be useful when he undertook long voyages. He married and settled down to family life, occasionally going on long voyages as the ship's physician. One of his voyages was upon the South Sea in a ship called the *Antelope*. A violent storm drove them to the north-west of Van Diemen's Land, dashing the ship against the rocks causing most of his shipmates to perish. Gulliver was washed ashore by the stormy waves and fell asleep exhausted. When he woke up he found that his arms, legs and hair had been tied down. There was a confused noise all round and he found many creatures resembling humans, of about six inches in height surrounding him. His loud shout frightened them and he could not understand their language. They shot little arrows at him even as he struggled to free himself. He convinced them that he was a peace-loving man. When he indicated to them that he was hungry, several ladders were placed at his side and they fed him great quantities of meat, and barrels of wine, all in miniature sizes. A messenger from the King spoke to Gulliver and said he had to be a prisoner and would be treated well. The carpenters and engineers among them worked tirelessly to produce the greatest carriage possible which could transport Gulliver. Gulliver was taken in the vehicle to an ancient temple, the largest in the kingdom which could house him. To transport Gulliver in the carriage, it required five hundred engineers, nine hundred workers, fifteen hundred horses and five hundred guards.

Glossary

physic	archaic usage to denote the practice or profession of medicine
Old Jury . . . Now called Old Jewry	name of a street in London
Mrs (Mary Burton)	in the seventeenth and eighteenth century, adult women, married or unmarried were referred to as Mrs (Mistress)
facility	ease
van Diemen's Land	now known as Tasmania
ligature	bandage
intrepid	fearless, courageous
Hekinah Degul *Tolgo phonic* *Langro Dehul*	Swift invents these words to represent the language of the Lilliputians
credentials	letters of introduction
signet Royal	royal seal of signature
hogshead	a large barrel or cask usually used to hold alcoholic beverages
ancient temple	reference to Westminster Hall where Charles I was condemned to death
soporific	a drug or substance capable of inducing sleep
edifice	a large imposing building

Comprehension

1. The original title of the book was *Travels into Several Remote Nations of the World.* Does this affect your view of the narrative?
2. Is there any evidence in the story that identifies it as fictional?
3. Gulliver is the narrator of the story. How effective do you think, is his narration? Do you begin to think of him as a character or as a pure narrator as you progress in the story?
4. Give a short description of Gulliver's life before he decided to undertake long voyages. Does his life on shore have any bearing on his life and decisions at sea?

5. Explain what happened to Gulliver after the storm.
6. How did Gulliver realise that he was imprisoned?
7. Describe the Lilliputians when Gulliver saw them for the first time.
8. How did they use their resources to imprison Gulliver?
9. How did the Lilliputians treat Gulliver initially?
10. Why did Gulliver tolerate them?
11. What evidence did Gulliver present in order to show that he was peace-loving and intended no harm?

Note: The first four questions have to be discussed repeatedly in the course of the narrative as your point of view may shift.

Part I: Chapter 2

Summary

The countryside looked like a garden with small fields, flower-beds and woods, and the town seemed a painted picture to Gulliver. At the order of the Emperor who was taller than his subjects by almost the 'breadth of Gulliver's nail,' enormous quantities of food and drink, by Lilliputian standards, were supplied to Gulliver. The Emperor personally supervised its dispensation. The council of ministers and the Emperor did consider starving or poisoning him but surmised that the huge rotting carcass would have caused a plague. Gulliver had been kind to several thugs who tormented him and did not give them any punishment except scaring them away. His magnanimity found favour with the King who decided to treat him well. More comforts were ordered for Gulliver, more persons were deputed to look after his needs and he was also taught their language. Gulliver's pockets were searched and the contents listed. Although the Lilliputians did not know the value or use of these items, they were taken away to be returned to him at a later date. Gulliver retained his spectacles and a pocket perspective (a small telescope) in a private pocket.

GLOSSARY

found myself on my feet	stood up
bridle	a harness fitted to a horse's head consisting of headstall, bit and reins
victuals	food
vials	small cylindrical vessels for holding medicine
durst	past tense of 'dare' in archaic dialect
at a draught	all in one gulp
deportment	bearing
smattering	slight knowledge of something
squall	scream
clemency	mercy
demesnes	land; domain
prodigious	surprisingly huge
not take it ill	to not be offended
fobs	small pockets for a watch in the waistband of trousers

COMPREHENSION

1. How does Gulliver describe the Lilliputian countryside?
2. Describe the general appearance and habits of the Emperor as presented in this chapter.
3. There is a well-known assumption that the Emperor may be the King, George I. Do you find any reason in the story for this?
4. Gulliver was shot at by the Lilliputians. How did he treat them? How did this help him?
5. What were the comforts given to Gulliver?
6. What were the precautions taken against Gulliver?
7. How did Gulliver show his friendly disposition and to what effect?

Part I: Chapter 3

Summary

Gulliver's gentleness and tolerance won the goodwill of the Emperor, court and the army. Even the people began to fear him less and were at ease in his company. Gulliver wanted his liberty and tried to win the friendship of the natives as he had learnt their language as well. He was entertained by the Emperor with several of the country shows, the most notable being that of the rope-dancers. Very often the ministers were also expected to undergo a trial of dexterity with sticks held by the Emperor over which they had to jump. They were appropriately rewarded with coloured silken threads, each colour denoting a particular status. Gulliver's petitions for liberty were acceded to by the King's court. He had to fulfil certain conditions prescribed by their laws which he agreed to and his chains were unlocked.

Glossary

diversions	pastimes
apprehensive	uneasy
dexterity	skill
memorial	something built in memory of people or institutions
rope dancers	besides the literal meaning, here it stands (allegorically)for political manipulations
Flimnap	generally believed to be Sir Robert Walpole, Whig politician and England's first Prime Minister. The capering or dancing on a tight-rope symbolises Walpole's dexterity in parliamentary tactics and political intrigues.
the King's cushions	may be a reference to one of the King's mistresses who helped Walpole rise to power after his fall in 1717

three fine threads	the distinction conferred by the King on his favourites is ridiculed – the order of the Garter (blue), the Order of the Thistle (green) and the Order of the Bath (red)
Skyresh Bolgolam	identified as the Earl of Nottingham

Comprehension

1. What were the amusements in the court of Lilliput? Describe them and the effect they had on Gulliver.
2. Identify the elements of satire in the Lilliputian court practices. Does Gulliver's height also become an object of satire?
3. What do you think are Swift's intentions in presenting these court practices?
4. Why was Bolgolam against Gulliver?
5. What is the parallel that Swift intends in this character?
6. How did Gulliver get his liberty?
7. How does the situation in Lilliput evoke similarities with the political atmosphere of England of Swift's time? Can you make any inferences from this chapter?
8. The story of Gulliver reads not only as an allegory but also as a simple tale of adventure. Can you substantiate this with examples?

Part I: Chapter 4

Summary

Gulliver's request to see Mildendo, the metropolis, was granted. The people of the town were informed of his visit. The windows were crowded with spectators who were asked to stay indoors for fear of being trampled upon. Gulliver went about his tour with great care. Shortly after his tour, he received a visit from the Principal Secretary of Private Affairs who briefed him about the struggling parties in the Empire (the Trarnecksan and Slamecksan identified by the high and low heels their shoes had). There was also a threat of invasion from the island of Blefuscu which was at war with Lilliput, the cause being the controversy over which end of an egg should be the more convenient to break – the big or the small end. Gulliver's help to defend the Emperor and state was sought and he readily agreed even though he did not want to interfere in the internal affairs of the country.

Note: The satire is on the kind of politics in which factions pursue their political agendas. Harold Bloom states that Lilliput is clearly England and the political parties – the Tories and the Whigs – are distinguishable only by the high or low heels of their shoes. The Lilliputian foreign policy, Bloom says, "parodies contemporary English policy towards France." The source is in the anecdote of the grandfather cutting his fingers when breaking an egg at the large end. An edict required thereafter, that eggs be broken at the small end. Rebellion ensued and the Big-Endians or Catholics moved to Blefuscu (France) and war was declared.

Glossary

sideling	(archaic usage) moving sideways, here to avoid destroying the houses on either side of the street
eave	edge of a roof
circumspection	caution
straggler	one who lags behind the rest
garret	a room on the top floor of a house
Tramecksan and Slamecksan	These names refer to the High and Low church parties – or the Tories and Whigs of Swift's time
animosity	enmity
intestine disquiets	internal differences
Blefuscu	fictional name here for France
edict	order proclaimed by authority
foment	to stir up trouble

schism	the division of a group into opposing parties due to a difference in beliefs
the heir to the crown	Prince of Wales (later George II) was opposed to the religious policy of his father. He favoured the Tories.
obstinate war	the wave of Spanish succession which lasted for thirteen years.
the larger end	The controversy between the Big Endians and the Little-Endians is a commentary on the religious controversy between the Roman Catholic and the Anglican Church. One Emperor lost his life and another his Crown. This refers to the execution of Charles I and the loss of his crown by James II. By the Test Act of 1673, all those holding office under the crown were obliged to take the sacrament according to the rites of the Anglican Church. The explanation is relevant to a critical interpretation of the satire and allegory in the book.

Comprehension

1. What were the precautions taken during Gulliver's tour of the metropolis of Mildendo. How did the people react?
2. What are the two evils referred to in the line, "We labour under two mighty evils".
3. Describe the nature of the "intestine disquiets" in Lilliput. What does this refer to?
4. Why did some Lilliputians migrate to Blefuscu?
5. What was cause of the war between Blefuscu and Lilliput?
6. Try to pinpoint the comic side of the court affairs of Lilliput.
7. How does the situation in Lilliput become a comment on the political scene in England at the time.

Part I: Chapter 5

Summary

Gulliver communicated his project of seizing the whole of the enemy's fleet consisting of about fifty men-of-war and a great number of vehicles which lay at anchor. Gulliver ordered for a great quantity of the strongest cable and bars of iron. Making strong hooks from these and attaching them to the cables, Gulliver walked to the fleet. The people of Blefuscu were terrified of his size and sudden appearance and fled. Gulliver drew the warships after him with ease. The Emperor of Lilliput praised his efforts by conferring upon him the highest title in the land and wanted Gulliver to help him conquer Blefuscu and enslave its people. Gulliver, however, refused and this displeased the Emperor and some of his ministers.

Note: "The Empire of Blefuscu is an island . . . . eight hundred yards wide". Details of direction and location give credibility to the narrative. Fiction has the appearance of fact. This is a feature of the travel narrative.

Glossary

intelligence	news
embargo	prohibitive order
warrant	written authority
puissant	powerful
"I would never be an instrument of bringing a free and brave people into slavery."	A reference to Swift's time where the Whigs wanted to continue the war until they could impose harsher terms upon France. The Tories worked for a settlement through negotiation.

Comprehension

1. Describe Blefuscu and its military strength.

2. What was Gulliver's project? How did he plan to execute it?
3. How did the enemy react to the plan?
4. Describe what happened in the Lilliput camp.
5. How was Gulliver rewarded?
6. What further designs did the Emperor have on Blefuscu and how was Gulliver involved?
7. Why did Gulliver refuse to help in the enslavement of the people of Blefuscu? What do you think of his views regarding freedom and tyranny?

Part I: Chapter 6

Summary

There was a private intrigue being formed against Gulliver. An influential courtier revealed the details of the plot which concerned Gulliver's honour and his life. Skyresh Bolgolam and Flimnap, the High Treasurer, had prepared articles of impeachment against Gulliver for treason and other capital crimes. Even as the Emperor supported Gulliver, they insisted on the death penalty. But the King in his benevolence decreed that the penalty should be reduced to the loss of his eyes and that he should gradually be starved to death by reducing his rations. Gulliver's first impulse was to resist and even destroy the metropolis. However, he remembered his promise to the Emperor and the favours he had received from him. Gulliver decided to leave Lilliput for Blefuscu, apparently innocent of the schemes being formed against him. He offered his services to the Emperor of Blefuscu who welcomed him warmly.

Glossary

intrigue	a secret plan to harm someone or cause some loss
salutations	greetings
conjunction	along with
obscured	not seen or heard clearly

articles	clauses of agreement
impeachment	accusation of treason
white staff	symbol of authority of the Lord Treasurer
extenuations	excuses
Only give order to put out both your eyes	may refer to what happened to Oxford and Bolingbroke. It was suggested that they should be accused of high misdemeanour, that is, unworthy behaviour, and not high treason. This would have entailed the forfeiture of their titles and estates instead of the death penalty.

Comprehension

1. How did Gulliver know of the private intrigue against him?
2. Why were Bolgolam and Flimnap against Gulliver?
3. Summarise the articles of impeachment. What was the Emperor's attitude?
4. What punishments awaited Gulliver? Were they justified?
5. What did Gulliver decide to do?
6. How did he leave Lilliput?
7. How did Blefuscu receive him?

Part I: Chapter 7

Summary

Sometime after his arrival in Blefuscu, Gulliver saw an upturned boat close to the coast. With the permission of the Emperor and the help of his men, Gulliver took some rope and other material to pull in and repair the boat. He requested the King to permit him to return to his own country. The King gave him the necessary help to fit his boat and enough food for the voyage. Gulliver also took some cattle and sheep with him and hay to feed them. He bade farewell to the King, his family and courtiers and set sail. After some time at sea, he saw an English merchant ship and called out to it. The captain was kind and took him on board. Gulliver soon reached home. He earned money exhibiting his cattle and sold them for a considerable profit before deciding to go on a voyage again.

Glossary

cordage	rope
descry	to catch sight of something that is difficult to discern clearly
My heart leapt within me	meaning that he was excited
raving	talking wildly

Comprehension

1. Describe what Gulliver saw as he walked about the coast of Blefuscu.
2. What action did he take to secure the boat? How would it be useful to him?
3. What was his request to the King?
4. How did he prepare himself for the voyage?
5. Was Gulliver able to take any inhabitants of the land with him and what instructions did he receive from the King in this regard?
6. Describe Gulliver's journey homeward. What were his experiences on board the ship?
7. Narrate the events that occurred after his return to England.

PART II: A VOYAGE TO BROBDINGNAG

Part II: Chapter 1

Summary

Two months after his return to his country, Gulliver set sail again in the *Adventure* bound for Surat. They had a good voyage and came in sight of a huge continent. The sailors and Gulliver set out to explore the land. Gulliver saw a huge creature in human form and ran away to hide in the grass that was twenty feet high. The countryside seemed fully cultivated. The stalks of corn in the corn field were forty feet high and the trees rose gigantic overhead. Gulliver saw another creature as tall as a church steeple and whose stride measured ten yards. Gulliver again tried to hide himself. He found it impossible to walk amidst the corn and was sure to be squashed to death. The reapers with their hooks and scythes seemed busy about the field. Just as Gulliver was trying to escape being caught, he was lifted by a large creature and held between thumb and forefinger. Staring at the creature he held, the farmhand understood Gulliver's supplicatory gestures and took him to his master, the farmer. The farmer took Gulliver home in a handkerchief. His wife was frightened on seeing him as at the sight of a toad or a spider. Dinner was served in huge vessels. Gulliver was terrified of falling off the table. Even the babies and the children seemed huge and monstrous to him. Gulliver was left in the care of the farmer's wife, who seeing that he was tired out, put him to bed.

Note: To Gulliver, everything in Brobdingnag was viewed from a telescope, a magnifying glass, just as he viewed things through a microscope in Lilliput.

Glossary

ague	a fever such as one from malaria that causes paroxysms of chills and sweating at intermittent intervals
computation	calculation

confound	confuse
supplicating posture	humble, pleading attitude
Brobdingnag	supposed to be an anagram of 'grand big noble'

Comprehension

1. What were Gulliver's experiences on the ship *Adventure?*
2. What were the experiences of the sailors after they landed?
3. What are the objects in the new land that Gulliver describes. What was the size and appearance of these objects? What was Gulliver's reaction to all this?
4. Why did Gulliver find it difficult to move in the cornfield?
5. How was Gulliver picked up by the farmhand? How did he escape a dreadful fate?
6. What treatment did Gulliver receive in the farmer's house?
7. 'Toad', 'spider', 'weasel' and 'plaything' – these are the images that signify Gulliver's size. What else do they suggest?
8. What were the objects that disgusted Gulliver? What do you think is the Swiftian comment on human beings and their ways?
9. Point out the contrast in the narrator's position moving from the land of dwarfs to the land of giants.
10. Can you identify the traces of satire and of fantasy in Gulliver's voyage to Brobdingnag?

Part II: Chapter 2

Summary

Gulliver was looked after by the farmer's nine-year-old daughter who made shirts for him, washed his clothes, made his bed, and instructed him in the language of the Brobdingnagians. Gulliver named her 'Glumdalclitch' or 'little nurse'. She dressed him up and looked after him as she would a doll. Gulliver too was grateful for her sympathetic attention. Word got around that the farmer had found a strange animal with fair skin, shaped like a human being in the fields. On the advice of the farmer's friend, Gulliver was taken to be an exhibit at the market place inn, the Sign of the Green Eagle. His antics fetched money and the farmer decided to take him to the metropolis. He hired a large room and Gulliver was shown to the populace ten times a day.

Glossary

splacnuck	Swift later explains that a splacnuck is "an animal in that country, . . . about six foot long"
hanger	a short sword usually hung from the belt
out of countenance	ruffled or flustered
fopperies	fashionably foolish pursuits
palisade	fence

Comprehension

1. Who looked after Gulliver in the farmer's house? What did the name given to the farmer's daughter signify?
2. What are the tasks Glumdalclitch does for Gulliver?
3. How was Gulliver treated by the farmer and his people?
4. Why was Gulliver made an 'exhibit'? What effect did this have on Gulliver? What is the satire intended here?
5. What do you think of Glumdalclitch? What kind of relationship does Gulliver share with her?
6. What is the author's purpose in presenting references to the human body that evoke disgust?

Part II: Chapter 3

Summary

Gulliver's master was avaricious for more money from more shows even though the strain was beginning to show on Gulliver who was reduced to a skeleton. Since the Queen wanted to see his antics, he was taken to the Court where Gulliver's humility pleased one and all. The Queen expressed a wish to have Gulliver live at the Court. The farmer sold Gulliver to the Queen and Glumdalclitch was retained to look after him. The Queen was so fond of Gulliver's company that she had a bed-chamber made for him, and a table placed upon her own table, beside her, where he was to dine. The King at first was eager to know about Europe, its way of life, religion, laws and politics. However, when he heard of the schisms and factions that constituted the government there, he was all in contempt for England, Gulliver's beloved country. The Queen's dwarf humiliated Gulliver by dropping him into a bowl of cream for which he was severely punished.

Glossary

unsatiable	not satisfied or gratified fully
vassal	a bondman, slave and dependant
giving great allowance	being liberal
copious	here, abounding in matter, thoughts or words
mortify	to humiliate, to wound the feelings of

Comprehension

1. Why did the farmer decide to sell Gulliver?
2. What was the kind of reception that Gulliver had from the ladies at Court?
3. What posture did he assume before the Queen? How did he impress the Queen?
4. Why did he want Glumdalclitch to remain with him?
5. What were the arrangements made for Gulliver's stay? Comment on this.
6. Comment on Gulliver's encounter with the King of Brobdingnag. What were the King's opinions about England after Gulliver's address? Comment on the author's intentions.

7. What was the dwarf's attitude to Gulliver? Describe the dwarf from Gulliver's point of view.
8. What did the dwarf do and how was he punished?

Part II: Chapter 4

Summary

The King's palace stood in Lorbrulgrud, the metropolis, a heap of buildings covering an area of roughly seven miles. Gulliver travelled with Glumdalclitch to see the town and the shops. He was put in a box specially made for the purpose and had a view of the chief temple, the countryside and also a horrible spectacle of the poverty-stricken and diseased in the market place.

Glossary

edifice	structure or building, usually one of an imposing size or appearance
cumbersome	inconvenient and burdensome in size

Comprehension

1. How is the King's palace described?
2. Describe Gulliver's journey to town.
3. What kind of box was made for Gulliver?
4. Why was Gulliver eager to see the chief temple? What were his reactions after seeing it?
5. What were the "humble spectacles" Gulliver was exposed to?

Part II: Chapter 5

Summary

Gulliver's small stature exposed him to several ridiculous and troublesome incidents. The malicious dwarf shook an apple tree as Gulliver stood below it and he was knocked down by a falling apple. A small dog sniffed him out while in the garden and carried him in his mouth to his master. Gulliver was terrified but he was not hurt. While enjoying the pastime of rowing, Gulliver had a minor fall and was saved by his nurse. The greatest danger came from a grinning and chattering monkey who seized him and took him to the roof top. Gulliver was saved after much effort and the monkey was killed. The King, the Queen, and the entire Court were much perturbed by this accident.

Glossary

malicious	having evil intentions
provocative	deliberately causing annoyance
out of hearing	a distance too far away to be heard
reprimand	to scold
gale	a moderate current of air between a stiff breeze and a hurricane
starboard, larboard	nautical terms that refer to the right and left of the vessel respectively of a person looking from stern to bow
officious	here, obligingly, dutifully
stomacher	a decorated triangle-shaped panel that fills in the front opening of a woman's gown or bodice
rabble	mob

Comprehension

1. What did Gulliver do to provoke the dwarf in the apple orchard?
2. How did the dwarf respond to Gulliver's taunting? How did this affect Gulliver?
3. What was the incident that happened to Gulliver while he was in the garden? Why was the incident hushed up?
4. How did the Queen show her concern for Gulliver's well-being?
5. Describe the accident which happened while rowing. How does Gulliver's size expose him to danger? How is this a source of fun to others?

6. Narrate Gulliver's experience with the monkey. Why was it "the greatest danger" he faced while at Brobdingnag?
7. What happened to the monkey?
8. How did the members of the court react to Gulliver's accident?

Part II: Chapter 6

Summary

The King desired that Gulliver should give him an exact account of the government of England so that he could use anything that deserved imitation for the good of his own country. Gulliver spoke of the fertility of the soil in England, and the climate of the country. He gave a lengthy speech as to how the English Parliament was constituted, its House of Lords and House of Commons. The Lords with their accomplishments proved to be the strength and support of the kingdom. They were aided by bishops, the spiritual fathers of the clergy and the people. The commoners were patriotic, wise men with great abilities. Gulliver also gave a description of the courts of justice and the treasury and ended with an account of England's history over the last hundred years. The King raised many queries about the Lords, the clergy and the commoners and concluded they were a quarrelsome people on account of the numerous wars they engaged themselves in. The history of the country, he felt, was replete with murders, revolutions avarice and excessive ambition. He concluded in disgust that Gulliver's was the "most pernicious race of little odious vermin that nature ever suffered to crawl upon the surface of the earth".

Glossary

ample patrimony	sufficient inheritance
bulwark	defensive wall
prostitute chaplains	The reference is to clergymen who abused their office for selfish gains

our generals must need be richer	may refer to Marlborough who Swift felt, prolonged the war with France to his material advantage
mercenary standing army	paid soldiers maintained in times of peace. In England, the Tories were opposed to this.
hypocrisy	a pretence of having a moral, desirable, or publicly approved attitude
perfidy	a deliberate breach of faith, treachery
panegyric	a formal public speech delivered in praise of a person or thing (here, country)
pernicious	causing insidious harm or ruin, deliberately hurtful
vermin	a term applied to animal species considered nuisances or pests

Note: This chapter and the next deal with English politics as seen through Gulliver's eyes.

Comprehension

1. What aspects of English institutions and life are described by Gulliver? How does the King react to these descriptions?
2. What were the queries, doubts and objections that the King had with reference to the House of Lords and the House of Commons?
3. What conclusions did the King draw from the account given of mercenaries, wars, and the country's history?
4. What aspects of England and its institutions are satirised in this chapter?
5. Do you think that Swift uses the King as his mouthpiece in this part of the story?
6. Do you think that Gulliver's voice is distinguishable from Swift's?
7. What was the King's final verdict on European social and political life?
8. How does this chapter become a satire on the moral nature of humanity?

Part II: Chapter 7

Summary

Gulliver continued to support his country, its governance and institutions. However, the King was disapproving and even contemptuous of all this. Gulliver attributed this to a narrowness of thinking, an insular education and even prejudice on the part of the King. Gulliver's offer to produce gunpowder which could destroy the metropolis horrified the King. He would have nothing to do with such "terrible engines". He was also totally against intrigue and politicking and valued the services of the farmer who produced food to sustain life.

Glossary

elude	to escape from something or someone especially by trickery
ingratiate	to bring oneself into favour with
grovel	to behave in a servile and humiliating manner
"And, he gave it for his opinion, that whoever could make two ears of corn . . . whole race of politicians put together"	A farmer by growing what is essential in life does greater service to humankind than a politician who wields power but has no intention to serve.

Comprehension

1. What are Gulliver's views of the King? Do you think that Swift is indirectly mocking at England through Gulliver? Substantiate your answer through a close reading of the text.
2. Comment on Gulliver's narration of the invention of gunpowder and its effects.

3. How does the King react to Gulliver's proposal? What does Gulliver think of the King's views?
4. What is the aim of the author in contrasting the King's views and Gulliver's opinions?
5. Are Gulliver's views on politics parallel with the author's own in this chapter? Why do you think so?

Part II: Chapter 8

Summary

Though Gulliver had endeared himself to the royal couple, he desired liberty because he wanted to be among his own people and live on equal terms. His deliverance came in an unusual manner. While sleeping in his box by the seaside, Gulliver found himself airborne (by an eagle presumably) and dropped into the sea. His box floated in the water and Gulliver was soon rescued by a ship. He was questioned by the captain and crew who released him from the box. Gulliver could not believe that he was among people of his own size. He told them of his unbelievable adventure and the captain asked him to write about it on his return to England. Gulliver took some time to adjust to the surroundings in his home country particularly with regard to size.

Glossary

impulse	sudden and uncontrollable action or feeling, not governed by reason
deliverance	freedom
hammock	a hanging bed made of canvas or netting, usually suspended between two trees or supports
veracity	truth

Comprehension

1. Paragraph one describes Gulliver's thoughts, aspirations and desires. Would you justify them and if so, on what grounds?

2. Describe the events that led to Gulliver's departure from Brobdingnag.
3. What happened to Gulliver when his box fell into the sea?
4. How was he rescued?
5. What did the captain do?
6. How did Gulliver behave upon his return home? How does this show that habit and prejudice are difficult to root out?

PART III: A VOYAGE TO LAPUTA, BALNIBARBI, LUGGNAGG, GLUBBDUBDRIB AND JAPAN

Part III: Chapter 1

Summary

Gulliver was invited to be surgeon of the ship *Hope-well*. During the voyage, pirates attacked the ship and the men were taken prisoners. The Japanese captain of one of the pirate ships took pity on Gulliver and gave him a canoe to set sail and some provisions to sustain him. Having been set adrift on the small canoe, Gulliver sailed past many islands and landed on one. As he sat on the rocks he saw a vast opaque body moving between him and the sun and coming towards the island. It was firm and bright with a flat bottom. With his pocket glass, Gulliver saw many people moving about on it as it descended parallel to him. It was a flying island. Gulliver made supplicating gestures to the people above in the hope of being admitted to the island. The people conferred among themselves and then let down a seat fastened to pulleys so that Gulliver could be conveniently drawn up.

Glossary

Laputa	stands for England (literal meaning 'a whore')

Fort St. George	a station of the East India Company in Madras (now Chennai)
sloop	a sailing vessel with a single mast
pinion	to restrain or tie down, usually one's arms
alliance	refers to the group consisting of England and Holland who were members of the Great Alliance against France
heathen	term used to refer to those not of Jewish or Christian faith
"I was sorry to find more mercy in a heathen, than in a brother Christian"	Gulliver's comment refers to mercy or kindness as characterising Christ and his followers. However, the sentence here indicates that it is a universal human trait and is not restricted to one sect.
reprobate	an immoral person
cadence	general inflection or modulation of voice

Note: This book, written after Book IV, is considered to be inferior to the other books and is a 'catch-all for satiric fragments which had no place in the other three parts'. The counter to this is that satire and its rhetorical device – irony, transcend the specifics of an era and are universal.

Comprehension

1. What happened to Gulliver's ship when it was struck by a storm? Compare the beginning of the voyage with the journey described in a 'A Voyage to Lilliput'.
2. Describe the Dutchman's attitude to Gulliver as opposed to that of the Japanese captain. What is Swift's satirical comment here?
3. How did the Dutch captain mete out punishment to Gulliver?
4. How did the Japanese captain help Gulliver?
5. How did Gulliver reach Laputa?
6. Describe the flying island and its people.

7. How did Gulliver manage to land safely there?

Part III: Chapter 2

Summary

Gulliver was filled with wonder at the Laputans who were rather strange in their shapes, habits and countenances. Their heads were all fixed either to the right or to the left, with one eye turned inwards and the other upwards. Their clothes had figures of celestial objects and musical instruments. Their servants always accompanied them and forced them into conversation by striking them upon the mouths and ears by means of flappers which were like bladders filled with pebbles. Otherwise they were so absorbed in the abstractions of mathematics and music and lived in constant fear of the earth being adversely affected by cosmic events. Even the King was deeply involved in a problem when Gulliver went to the palace to meet him. The Laputans were always worried about dangers that threatened them and therefore they hardly slept or enjoyed life and its simple pleasures.

Glossary

cogitate	to think or ponder
concourse	a crowd
disquietude	state of anxiety, unrest
effluvia	a residual emanation of gas or vapour
hobgoblin	an ugly, mischievous elf

Comprehension

1. Describe the physical appearance and dress of the Laputans.
2. Who were the flappers and what was their function?
3. What evidence do you find in this chapter to suggest that the Laputans were not practical people?

4. What fears did the Laputans have regarding their future?
5. Describe how the Laputans greeted each other every morning and what do you infer from their behaviour?
6. Do you think the Laputans are presented as comic or tragic creatures? Discuss.
7. What is the target of Swift's satire in this chapter? Is exaggeration one of the techniques he employs to invoke laughter?

PART III: CHAPTER 3

SUMMARY

The floating island of about ten thousand acres depended on a huge loadstone to lift itself up and bring it down and move from one place to another. An oblique motion took it to different parts of the King's dominion. The King controlled his subjects by various means if there was any mutiny or rebellion. He would station his island above the offending town or district thus depriving them of sun and rain. Stones would be thrown on them from above, and if the rebellion persisted, he would let the island crush them. The latter step was not usually taken as it would make the King vastly unpopular and most of his ministers had their estates down there and did not wish to incur any damage. The monarch had great powers but the people below did not want to be the King's enslaved subjects.

GLOSSARY

adamant	a stone once believed to be impenetrable in its hardness
loadstone	a piece of iron used as a magnet
oblique	slanting
insurrection	open revolt against civil authority or any constituted government

COMPREHENSION

1. Describe the floating island and its unique features. What were its limitations?
2. Why did the estate owners refuse to form a ministry?
3. What were the measures of punishment that the King threatened to take in order to make his subjects obey him?
4. How did the King's control of the island affect the lands below?
5. Is the relationship between Laputa and the lands below a reflection of the England-Ireland relationship? How is the satire accomplished?

PART III: CHAPTER 4

SUMMARY

Since Gulliver was not well-versed in mathematics or music in which the knowledge of the Laputans was superior, he was held in contempt and was ignored. Gulliver interacted only with common people such as women, tradesmen, flappers, and court pages. He wanted to leave the island and therefore sought the help of a Great Lord who obtained permission for him from the King. Gulliver was to go to Lagado. He was treated well and shown around. He saw the beautiful country, the grain fields, the vineyards, meadows and well-built houses. However, the scientists from the Academy of Projectors changed all this. Their projects were radically different from previous approaches. They left their schemes incomplete and as a result most of the country lay waste and the houses lay in ruins.

GLOSSARY

contemptible	worthy of contempt, i.e, to have no regard for
illustrious person	famous individual (here used ironically)
grandee	great Lord

patent	refers to the exclusive right granted by the government to the inventor to make use of, create and sell a particular invention or process for a fixed period of time.
caprice	an inclination to change one's mind impulsively
Academy of Projectors	an allegorical account of the Royal Society in London and similar institutions. Swift satirises the experiments conducted in these institutions.
contrive	to carefully plan and calculate, devise or formulate

Comprehension

1. Why was Gulliver treated with disdain by the Laputans?
2. How did he go to Balnibarbi? Who helped him go away?
3. Describe the sights Gulliver saw there. What kind of people did he see?
4. How and why does Swift satirise the scientific experiments in agriculture practised by the Laputans?
5. What was the result of the feud among the Laputans?
6. What did the Academy of Projectors do and how did its work affect society?

Part III: Chapter 5

Summary

Gulliver visited the Academy of Projectors where scientists were involved in conducting various experiments which included extracting sunbeams from cucumbers, reducing human excrement to its original food, and calcine ice into gunpowder. A 'clever' architect was trying to build houses starting from the roof and working down to the foundation. A blind man and his apprentices were mixing colours by feeling and smelling them. Other experiments included using hogs to plough the fields and obtaining silk thread from cobwebs. There were strange experiments being conducted in the mathematical school too.

Glossary

meagre aspect	here refers to a thin, possibly poorly fed and clothed body
hermetically sealed	airtight closure
inclement	stormy or severe
ingenuity	the quality of being inventive and resourceful
daubed over	covered or smeared with, here filth
tincture	a trace or tinge of some substance
scum off	to remove
treatise	a systematic and extensive written discourse upon a particular subject of study
malleable	adaptable, capable of being formed or shaped
prudent	practical and wise, exercising good judgement
glutinous matter	matter possessing the nature of glue: sticky substance
cephalic	relating to the head
bolus	a single relatively large quantity of substance such as a dose of a drug administered orally and usually for therapeutic purposes
abstinence	act or practice of abstaining from indulging in an appetite

Comprehension

1. Do you think Swift is ridiculing the projects of the Academy? What is his intention? What is he satirising?

2. Describe the nature of the projects. Comment on their practicality. Is there a touch of the absurd in these projects?
3. What were the experiments conducted by the "ingenious architect" and the man born blind?
4. Discuss the experiments in agriculture and their feasibility as you see it.
5. Read the experiments in the Academy as against current technological advances. Does it change your opinion of the experiments conducted by the academy?

Part III: Chapter 6

Summary

Gulliver decided to leave Laputa and set out for Luggnagg. However, a ship bound for Luggnagg was not readily available and he was persuaded to take a trip to the little island of Glubbdubdrib in the company of a gentleman and his friend. This island was inhabited by magicians and sorcerers. The Governor of the island and his family were served by servants whom they could call from the dead. Gulliver too managed to see, on request, Homer and Aristotle and some English country gentlemen. He felt that they were far superior to the contemporary corrupt generation.

Glossary

necromancy	black magic
Homer	Ancient Greek poet who authored the epics *Iliad* and *Odyssey*
Aristotle	a great Greek philosopher of the 4th century B.C. who wrote the *Poetics*
comely	attractive, of a pleasing and wholesome appearance
visage	countenance, facial expression
lank	long, straight and limp, here used to refer to hair

antiquity	here, refers to ancient times
lineament	a distinctive contour, shape or line of the face
unbraced	to weaken or make slack
sallow	a sickly and yellowish pallor or complexion
rancid	repugnant, smelling of staleness
comely	attractive, of a pleasing and wholesome appearance
stamp	a distinctive mark or impression, here left by the yeomen of ancient England

Comprehension

1. Explain the significance of the name Glubbdubdrib with reference to this chapter.
2. Describe the peculiar features of the island.
3. What was the technique used by the Governor to get his work done?
4. Why did Gulliver want to see the ancients? What were his impressions?
5. Why were Homer and Aristotle "two perfect strangers to the rest of the company"? Explain the irony.
6. What were Gulliver's conclusions on comparing the living and the dead?

Part III: Chapter 7

Summary

From Glubbdubdrib, Gulliver sailed to Luggnagg, a dangerous voyage. He posed as a Dutchman since the Dutch were the only Europeans admitted to Japan and Gulliver wished to travel to that country. His credentials were verified and he was finally allowed to meet the King, and for this he had to lick the dust before his footstool. Gulliver found the Luggnaggians generous and courteous. He was taken to meet the Struldbruggs or

Immortals, a breed peculiar to their country. A child born with a red mark on his/her forehead was destined to be immortal. Gulliver was delighted with this information and thought that if he were to be born a Struldbrugg he would be an oracle and a living treasury of knowledge and wisdom. The Luggnaggians explained that this was far from the case. The Struldbruggs were like mortals till the age of thirty but later as they grew older they grew peevish and withdrawn and cut themselves off from all pleasure. They suffered loss of memory, were unemployable, became ugly and handicapped and were considered 'dead' at eighty. Gulliver lost his desire for immortality on seeing the miserable state of the immortals who were without eternal youth.

Glossary

cast anchor	to secure a vessel at sea to the seabed, usually at a port or close to the shoreline
treachery	violation of trust
inadvertence	negligence
plausible	reasonable, likely to be true
retinue	a body of retainers and attendants accompanying an important parsonage such as a King or a Lord
calamity	a disaster, an event that brings loss, lasting distress and severely affects those involved
imbecile	silly or stupid person
perpetuity	the quality of being for ever
infirmities	bodily ailment and weakness usually brought on by old age
opinionative	dogmatic in one's opinions
peevish	irritable, easily annoyed
covetous	greedy, avaricious
morose	melancholic or of a gloomy disposition
dotage	feeble minded senility
pittance	very small monetary allowance

Comprehension

1. Why did Gulliver hide his identity and pose as a Dutchman?
2. What kind of people were the Luggnaggians? What was their court style of honouring a guest?
3. Who were the Struldbruggs? How were they identified?
4. How did Gulliver react to the idea of immortality?
5. Describe the immortals, their appearance, and the condition of their mind and intellect.
6. How did Gulliver's glorious ideas about immortality get shattered after his experience with the Struldbruggs?
7. What does this chapter reveal about mortality, youth and the meaning of life? Point out the satire that Swift employs.

Part III: Chapter 8

Summary

Gulliver left Luggnagg with letters from the King to the Emperor of Japan. The King also gave Gulliver some gold and a red diamond which he later sold in England for a large sum. Gulliver's ship reached Xamoschi, Japan. The customs officers saw the letter and Gulliver was received as a public minister. He was taken to be a Hollander and his letter was explained to the Emperor. Gulliver left Yedo and soon fell into the company of some Dutch sailors. It was a safe voyage to Amsterdam from where Gulliver left for England. After five and half years on the high seas, Gulliver was reunited with his family.

Comprehension

1. What kind of gifts did Gulliver receive from the King of Luggnagg? What did he do with them?
2. How did Gulliver reach Japan? Describe his experiences in that country.
3. Describe Gulliver's voyage back to England and his reunion with his family.

PART IV: A VOYAGE TO THE COUNTRY OF THE HOUYHNHNMS

Part IV: Chapter 1

Summary

Gulliver again set sail in the *Adventure*, this time as a navigator and not as a surgeon. His recruits from Barbados turned out to be rogues who threw him out of the ship. However, with the help of a long-boat Gulliver reached a country where the creatures were singular and deformed–hirsute creatures with sharp, hooked claws which enabled them to climb trees. They ran away when they saw two horse – like creatures approaching. Gulliver found that the two horses behaved like people discussing important matters. He had many conjectures about them and spoke to them but they could not understand him. Gulliver learnt from them the word 'Yahoo' pronounced like the neighing of a horse and also the word 'Houyhnhnm'.

Glossary

calenture	a tropical delirious fever formerly thought to be caused by the heat
conspiracy	plot
long-boat	the longest boat carried on a merchant ship
necessaries	all that is necessary to maintain a particular life style or in this case, a voyage
strand	foreshore
circumspect	in a cautious manner
frizzle	small tight curl
lank	long, straight and usually limp
antipathy	dislike
manifest tokens of wonder	expressing curiosity and astonishment
articulate	expressing oneself clearly in distinct meaningful words and syllables
deliberate on	to think about something or to consider what to do about someone or something

affair of weight	matter of importance
judicious	refers to having or proceeding from good judgement
metamorphose	to transform into something wholly different
conjecture	an inference or judgement based on inconclusive evidence
perceive	to begin to be aware directly through the senses, of sight usually
orthography	the art of writing words with the proper letters according to accepted usage and spelling
Houyhnhnms	refers to the race of horses here. The Houyhnhnms are a race endowed with reason and noble qualities.

Comprehension

1. In what capacity did Gulliver join the *Adventure* crew?
2. What circumstances led Gulliver to the land of the Houyhnhnms?
3. What sight greeted Gulliver soon after he landed? How did he react to it?
4. What were the horses doing? What did Gulliver think of them and why?
5. How did the horses respond to Gulliver?
6. What was the nature of their language? Illustrate with examples from the text.
7. Do you think this chapter contains fairy-tale elements or absurdities? Explain.

Part IV: Chapter 2

Summary

Gulliver was taken to a long building made of timber and covered with straw. A rack and manger extended the whole length on one side. The horse neighed with authority and the grey horse answered in the same dialect. 'Yahoo' was a word that was repeated and Gulliver was exposed to the hateful creatures he had met on arrival and their detestable habits. Gulliver was horrified to observe on close encounter that these creatures resembled humans. The horses found it difficult to differentiate the Yahoos from Gulliver. Through signs Gulliver managed to get milk to appease his hunger. He also had oats and was occasionally able to catch a rabbit or bird and pick some wholesome herbs which he ate as a salad to go with his oatmeal bread. He slept in the stable.

Glossary

wattle	refers to a construction of poles intertwined with twigs or branches and used for the roofs, walls or fences.
dialect	a regional or social variety of language differing markedly from the standardised form
sit on haunches	to sit with one's hind quarters resting on one's heels
rack	framework with bars
manger	long open trough for horses to eat from
detestable	hateful
withes	a tough supple twig mostly used for binding things together
sorrel nag	light reddish horse
abominable	detestable, loathsome and disgusting
fetlock	part of the back of horse's leg above the hoof. Here the Houyhnhnm offers Gulliver a fetcock full of oats, or in human terms—a handful.
winnow	the process of separating the chaff from the grain
insipid	flavourless

COMPREHENSION

1. Does this chapter draw our attention to the human–animal relationship? Describe Gulliver's encounter with the horses here in this chapter.
2. Why does Swift focus on the disgusting habits of the Yahoos?
3. How did Gulliver manage his dinner on the first day?
4. How did the 'master horse' show his concern for Gulliver?
5. What were the food arrangements that Gulliver could make for himself with the help of the master horse?
6. Draw pen portraits of the Yahoos and the Houyhnhnms as visualised in this chapter.

PART IV: CHAPTER 3

SUMMARY

Gulliver was eager to learn the language of the Houyhnhnms. A sorrel nag taught him to speak the language well. This enabled Gulliver to explain to the Houyhnhnms about his land. However, he always remained fully clothed for fear of being mistaken for a Yahoo who resembled humans. Since Yahoos were odious animals, he did not want to be mistaken for them in any case. Gulliver on being questioned revealed everything about life in England. He dwelt at length on how horses were treated in England, and how they are kept by the rich and by the common people. His master showed resentment at the treatment meted out to Houyhnhnms in England. The master was also disapproving of the manner in which people indulged in crime and vice. He wanted to know more about England and about Gulliver himself.

GLOSSARY

prodigy	person or child with exceptional abilities
appellation	title or designation
tractable	easily handled

vicious	spiteful, bad tempered
castrate	to deprive of vigour by removing the testicles of, to geld
intemperance	the indulgence of an appetite or passion, also refers to an excessive intake of alcoholic beverages

Comprehension

1. How did Gulliver learn the language of the Houyhnhnms and why was this important to him?
2. There is a discussion here regarding clothes. Why is Gulliver keen on maintaining a distinction between him and the Yahoos?
3. Explain Gulliver's master's perception of this problem.
4. Summarise Gulliver's account of life in England.
5. What was his master's reaction to the description provided by Gulliver of the human–horse relationship?
6. Comment on the narrative in this chapter. Is the description realistic, absurd or fictive and satirical?

Part IV: Chapter 4

Summary

Gulliver related in detail the nature, reasons and the results of war in England. The motives for war included ambition, the corruption of ministers, and differences in opinions even on petty matters. Millions of Yahoos were killed as a result. This information bewildered his master. His perplexity deepened when Gulliver told him how the law could ruin people. Lawyers were so used to falsehood that they could never argue for true justice, and that judges acted according to those in power. Gulliver also revealed that money could perform any feat in Yahoo land and that the lack of it led people to rob, cheat, steal, pimp and whore as the case may be. The master was totally at a loss to understand this phenomenon.

Glossary

Revolution	refers to the glorious revolution or bloodless revolution of 1688. This brought Mary and William of Orange to the throne.
Prince of Orange	William of Orange began a war with France. The campaign continued with the Duke of Marlborough as general. France was defeated and the treaty of Utrecht was signed in 1714.
Yahoos	term used almost as a synonym for humans.
"Difference in opinion hath cost many millions of lives"	The allusions here are to the controversies in the Church over transubstantiation (the Christian belief that the bread used during mass becomes the flesh of Christ), church music, use of images in worship, and the use of church vestments
bench	judges
hector	to dominate or intimidate in a blustering way, to bully

Comprehension

1. Explain the causes of war among human society as put forth by Gulliver.
2. Is Swift satirising the practice of war among humankind? What are the master's reactions?
3. Explain "that the *law* which was intended for *every* man's preservation should be any man's ruin." How does Gulliver counter this?
4. Point out the ironical implications of law and its practice in human society.
5. How does Swift use Gulliver as his mouthpiece to criticise and satirise European wars, the legal system and human nature?

PART IV: CHAPTER 5

SUMMARY

Gulliver began to see the many virtues of the Houyhnhnms and naturally his eyes opened to the contrast with human corruption. He so admired these creatures that he would have opted to spend the rest of his life among them if he could. He tried to protect himself and his own country against the astute observations of his master who saw human beings as animals without an iota of reason. In his master's account of the Yahoos, they were portrayed as savage brutes and gluttons, always engaged in a terrible civil war. They had obnoxious ways, and on one occasion Gulliver was assaulted by a female Yahoo who mistook him for one of her kind when he was bathing in the river. The Houyhnhnms, however, were endowed with virtues such as friendship and benevolence and from childhood learnt temperance, industry, exercise and cleanliness. They were totally occupied with the welfare of the country and the well-being of the young.

GLOSSARY

detest	hate
extenuate	to lessen the magnitude of faults or crimes by taking the situation into consideration
venerate	respect
repletion	a state of excessive fullness due to overeating
diversion	amusement
temperance	refers to moderation and self restraint expressed in behaviour or expression
industry	habitual diligence in any pursuit as opposed to idleness
vernal equinox	springtime when the sun crosses the equator, and day and night are equal
maxim	general truth

Comprehension

1. What was the effect that experience with the Houyhnhnms had on Gulliver?
2. Explain the line, "I extenuated their faults". Do you think that Gulliver is being truthful? Base your answer upon the information that Gulliver imparts to his master regarding the European nations and England in particular.
3. What are the features of the Yahoos? In what ways did they resemble human beings?
4. Describe Gulliver's encounter with the female Yahoo. What does this indicate?
5. What qualities of the Houyhnhnms did Gulliver find praiseworthy?
6. What lessons did the Houyhnhnms learn from childhood?
7. Why do you think Gulliver praises the race of quadrupeds?
8. Give a sentence that implies that the Yahoos represent the bestial human and the Houyhnhnms, a person's nobler nature. What grounds would you use to substantiate this?

Part IV: Chapter 6

Summary

In the General Assembly it was debated whether the Yahoos should be destroyed. Gulliver's master gave him a vivid account of what transpired at the Assembly. The Yahoos were considered the most filthy, noisy and deformed animals of nature that had accidentally stumbled into their country. The Houyhnhnms on the other hand were traditional, cultured beings leading simple lives. They lived close to nature and faced every experience with equanimity, dying eventually, not of disease but of old age.

Glossary

exterminate	destroy, remove
allege	to assert to be true without proof
pastern	part of horse's foot between the back of the leg and hoof

exalted	lofty, elevated or sublime
dexterity	skill and grace in physical movement, especially when using one's hands

Comprehension

1. What was the main point of the debate in the General Assembly?
2. What were the arguments in favour of destroying the Yahoos? Is Swift suggesting a similar fate for humans?
3. What were the skills possessed by the Houyhnhnms? In what ways were they superior to the Yahoos and the humans?
4. Do you think that Swift employs satire in his depiction of the Yahoos and the Houyhnhnms?

Part IV: Chapter 7

Summary

Gulliver had settled down comfortably and happily in the land of the Houyhnhnms. His physical needs of food, clothing and shelter were more than satisfied and he enjoyed great peace of mind with no conflicts or betrayals. Gulliver visited many illustrious Houyhnhnms and learnt much from them. He realised his own ugliness and pettiness. However, the Great Assembly decided that he had to leave the land as his Yahoo-like appearance was suspect. Gulliver was grief-stricken. However, he made his own canoe and left with the usual formalities, bidding farewell to his master and the other Houyhnhnms. That was the end of his stay with the Houyhnhnms.

Glossary

maxim: "necessity is the mother of invention"	a standard proverb that means that when human beings are in need of something, they try their best to devise ways to satisfy the need

discourse	a lengthy verbal exchange or discussion on a particular subject
minion	an obsequious and servile follower who uses flattery to find favour and therefore becomes a favourite
informer	spy
auditor	listener
perplex	confuse
hempen threads	thread made of the tough coarse fibre of the cannabis plant
prostrate	to throw oneself flat on the ground in submission or adoration

Comprehension

1. What were the factors in the land of the Houyhnhnms that made Gulliver comfortable and happy? Show through examples how Swift uses Gulliver's voice to portray humour and satire.
2. Why was Gulliver asked to leave? How did it affect him?
3. Describe the preparations he made for his departure.
4. What was Gulliver's state of mind on taking his leave of his master and the family?

Part IV: Chapter 8

Summary

Gulliver reached New Holland safely as there were no storms or mishaps at sea. His initial plan was to discover some small island which would provide him with the basic necessities of life so that he did not have to worry about those and could spend some quiet time contemplating the virtues of the Houyhnhnms. On the fourth day, he was chased by savage natives and wounded. He decided to stay in the island and tolerate the barbarians rather than go back to be at the mercy of European Yahoos. A ship came to his rescue, and the sailors took him on board. They laughed at his speech which was like the neighing of a horse. To Gulliver, their speech appeared monstrous and unnatural. The captain Pedro de Mendez offered him clothes, but Gulliver refused the 'Yahoo' attire. Gulliver returned to England but found that he could not re-adjust to the situation at home because it was so different from life in the Houyhnhnm country. His wife and children now appeared unbelievably hateful to him. In order to feel at home, he preferred to keep two stone horses in his stable for whatever company they could offer him.

Glossary

inimitable	that which cannot be imitated
New Holland	Australia
canoe	a light open boat that can be propelled by paddles and has pointed ends
conjecture	conclude
cranny	a crevice, a narrow opening usually on a rock surface or a wall
lurking-hole	here, refers to a hole in which a person can possibly hide
gratis	free of cost
abhor	to detest or regard with loathing
defile	to corrupt, to make impure or unclean
alliance	here, a relationship based on kinship, marriage or common interest
bridle	the harness of a horse used to control or restrain it

Comprehension

1. How did Gulliver finally land on the island of New Holland?
2. What was the first shocking encounter that Gulliver had on this island?
3. Why do you think Gulliver says that he prefers the savages to civilised men? Base your answer upon his description of the savages and his experiences in the land of the Houyhnhnms.
4. What kind of man was de Mendez?

5. Do you think that Gulliver is a misanthrope? Does he reflect Swift's views?
6. Describe Gulliver's strange behaviour at home. What do you think are the reasons for this?
7. Bring out the irony of Gulliver's reactions when he returns home.

Part IV: Chapter 9

Summary

Gulliver was unable to tolerate the sight and behaviour of the English Yahoos. He was all admiration for the Houyhnhnms and hoped to instruct his family about their virtues. He felt he could not tolerate humanity's pride and would not allow any person with this absurd vice to come near him.

Glossary

docible	teachable, easily taught and managed
habituate	to get accustomed to something by frequent exposure
rue	a strongly scented shrub used in the Mediterranean region
lavender	a plant with purple flowers whose oil is used to make perfumes
reconcilement	to bring oneself to accept
tincture	trace

Comprehension

1. What task did Gulliver take upon himself? Why did he do so?
2. Why does Gulliver now find human beings including his wife and family hateful when he returns to England? Explain. What is Gulliver's chief grouse or complaint against the Yahoo race?

CRITICAL ESSAYS

1. *Gulliver's Travels*

By Maynard Mack

That Swift's greatest satire, *Gulliver's Travels*, is sometimes relegated to the nursery can be explained in part by the fact that most adults are unwilling to face the truth about themselves.

Gulliver, who is Swift's *persona* in this work, is more complex and more complexly used than the assumed identities we have met in the *Argument* and the *Modest Proposal*. He is, first of all, a stolid unemotional, but candid and reliable observer. In this respect, his account has been made to resemble those of the authentic voyagers of Swift's time, whose narratives of distant lands (it was the last great age of exploration) were devoured by Augustan readers. Voyages, both authentic and imaginary, were in fact one of the prominent literary genres. The intent of the imaginary voyages was almost always to satirize the existing European order, and it did so by playing up the innocence, manliness, and high ethical standards of the untutored peoples whom the voyager claimed to have met. But the real voyages also, even those recounted by missionaries and priests, pointed to the same conclusion. Reflecting, without realizing it, the general modern rehabilitation of "nature" (in contrast to the older view of nature as fallen and in need of redemption), all these voyages tended alike to stress the goodness of unspoiled primitive man. The human nature presented in such accounts (and in a substantial tradition of other writings ranging from Montaigne to Rousseau) did not appear to be morally unreliable, or controllable only by the disciplines of civilization. On the contrary, it was evidently instinctively good, and had been corrupted by civilization; if these corrupting influences could be removed, there was practically no limit to its perfectibility.

Swift, whose aim in *Gulliver* is (among other things) to show the fatuity of this creed, deliberately adopts the voyage genre of the enemy and turns it to his own ends. Wherever Gulliver goes among his fantastic aborigines, he is always encountering, instead of handsome and noble savages, aspects of man as he perennially is, whether in civilized society or in nature. Among the Lilliputians, it is human pettiness, especially moral pettiness, and the triviality of many of the forms, titles, customs, pretenses, and "points of honour" by which men assert their dignity and about which they conduct their quarrels. Characteristically, the devices Gulliver meets with in this country are those of little men: pomposity; intrigue, and malice. Among the Brobdingnagians, on the other hand, it is the physical grossness of the human species, its callous indifference to what it flings aside or tramples underfoot: "For I apprehended every moment that he would dash me against the ground, as we usually do any hateful little animal which we have in mind to destroy." In this country, Gulliver is constantly being appalled by circumstances of coarseness; the nurse's monstrous breast, the linen "coarser than sackcloth," the Queen crunching "the wing of a lark, bones and all, between her teeth," and drinking "above a hogshead at a draught" — or else of callused contempt: the schoolboy's hazelnut, the farmer's indifference to Gulliver's fatigue, the pet lamb promised to Glumdalclitch but casually dispatched to the butcher. At the same time (for in this voyage the satire cuts two ways), Gulliver's conversation with the King throw a frightful light on man as civilized European.

The fourth voyage brings us the Yahoos and the animal nastiness that is also one aspect of the human situation. The Yahoos are Swift's climactic answer to the contemporary infatuation with noble "natural" men; and the language used of them becomes especially vulgar and anatomical to indicate the repulsiveness of "unspoiled" nature, either physical or moral. But the Yahoos are also something more. We may see embodied in them that extreme view of man as hopelessly irrational, decadent, and depraved, which extreme Puritanism fostered in religious terms, and which had been exemplified in nonreligious terms by Hobbe's portrait of life in a state of nature as "nasty, brutish, and short." This view, it will be observed, Swift embodies in the Yahoos only to reject it. Though Gulliver makes the error of identifying himself and other human beings completely with the Yahoos, we and Swift do not. Nor do we take the ideal life for man, as Gulliver does, to be the tepid rationality of the horses. Reacting against the Yahoos because he mistakes the animal part of human nature which they represent for the whole, Gulliver goes to the other extreme and worships pure rationality in the Houyhnhnms, which is likewise only a part of the whole. Neither extreme answers to the actual human situation, and Swift, despite the persistence with which this voyage has been misinterpreted, is careful to show us this. That Gulliver's self-identification with the Yahoos is mistaken, we realize (if we have not realized it long before) as soon as we see Gulliver insisting that his wife and children are Yahoos, and preferring to live in the stable. Similarly, we see the mistakenness of his desire to be like the Houyhnhnms as soon as we pause to reflect that they are horses: Swift has used animals as his symbols here in order to make it quite plain that pure rationality is not available to *man*—would make us absurd, monstrous, and tedious as the Houyhnhnms. For the truth, as we are meant to realize, is that man is neither irrational physicality like the Yahoos nor passionless rationality like the Houyhnhnms; neither (to paraphrase Swift's own terms in a famous letter to Pope) *animal implume bipes* nor animal *rationale*, but *animal rationis capax*.

And now, if we look back again at the voyages, we can see that this middle view has been the theme from the very beginning. In Lilliput, the vices and trivialities of the little people are seen against the normal humanity and benevolence of Gulliver. In Brobdingnag, over against Gulliver's unconscious brutality in recommending gunpowder and the description of Europeans as "the most pernicious race of little odious vermin that nature ever suffered to crawl upon the face of the earth," Swift shows us the magnanimity of the King and the tenderness of Glumdalclitch. Even in the last and darkest voyage, we are never allowed to suppose (witness the Portuguese sea-captain) that real human beings are the detestable creatures Gulliver supposes them. Man is fallen so far as Swift is concerned, and the new notions of natural goodness and infinite perfectibility are nonsense; but man is also—to put it in the nonreligious terms that Swift has chosen for his parable—capable of regeneration: *rationis capax*.

Swift's instrument in this blending of light and shadow is the assumed identity, Gulliver. Through Gulliver, Swift is able to deliver the most powerful indictment of man's inhumanity ever written in prose, and at the same time to distinguish his own realistic view of man's nature from the misanthropy of which he has sometimes been accused. While Gulliver is still naïve, mainly in the first two voyages, satire can be uttered through him, he himself remaining unaware of it. Later, when he begins to fall into misanthropy, still more corrosive satire can be uttered by him. But in the end, satire is uttered of him, and we see his mistake. For we discover, if we look closely, that all through the fourth voyage Gulliver is represented as becoming more and more like a horse—learning to neigh, to walk with an equine gait, to cherish the ammoniac smell. He is represented, in other words, as isolating himself from mankind, and it is only this isolation in its climactic form that we see in his treatment of his family and his residence in the stables at the close. To suppose, as many careless critics have done, that Swift is recommending this as an *ideal* for man is the consequence of the fatal error mentioned earlier—of identifying the author of an Augustan work with its *persona*.

From *Swift: A Collection of Critical Essays.*
Ed. Ernest Tuveson (NJ: Prentice Hall Inc), 1967.

2. Gulliver's Voyage to the Houyhnhnms

Kathleen Williams

It has long been recognized that the fourth Voyage of *Gulliver's Travels,* far from being the outburst of a misanthrope who delighted in 'degrading human Nature', is the culmination of Swift's lifelong attack on the pride of man, especially the pride which convinces him that he can live by the light of his unaided reason, the pride that Swift himself sums up, in the title of one of his imaginary discourses in *A Tale of A Tub,* as 'An Universal Rule of Reason, or Every Man his own Carver'. In particular he is taking up a position opposed to the doctrines of natural goodness which pervade eighteenth-century thought and which find systematic expression in the writings of 'Toland, Collins, Tindal, and others of the fraternity', who, as Swift remarks, all talk much the same language and whose ideas are dismissed in the *Argument against Abolishing Christianity* as 'Trumpery'. It is clear, both from the satires and the religious writings, that Swift was hostile to all doctrines of the natural self-sufficiency of man, whether they were expressed in Deistic terms or in the related pride of neo-Stoicism; and the Fourth Voyage of *Gulliver's Travels* embodies that hostility. But while the object of attack is established, it is not immediately clear, from the Voyage itself, whether any positive position is implied in the Houyhnhnms or in the other characters. The Yahoos, clearly, embody the negative intention, and are to be condemned. This is what happens to man when he tries to live by reason and nature; he falls, as has been pointed out, into a 'state of nature' nearer to that envisaged to Hobbes than that of Locke's *Two Treatises of Government*. It is significant that, according to one Houyhnhnm theory, the Yahoos were descended from a pair of human beings, driven to the country by sea: 'coming to Land and being forsaken by their Companions, they retired to the Mountains, and degenerating by Degrees, became in Process of Time, much more savage than those of their own Species in the Country from whence these two Originals came'. Presumably these originals, forced into self-reliance, had degenerated because their feeble human reason had been overwhelmed by an irrational 'nature', and more adequate guides had been forgotten.

The ambiguity of the fourth Voyage lies not in the Yahoos, but in the positions of Gulliver and, especially, of the Houyhnhnms. The function of the Houyhnhnms may be to present an ideal of the true life of reason, to be admired even if unattainable, and to be contrasted with the Yahoos to chasten the pride of that lump of deformity, man, by showing him the vanity of his pretensions. But if Swift did intend the Houyhnhnms to stand as an ideal contrast, he has badly mismanaged the matter. The Houyhnhnms do not strike the reader as altogether admirable beings; indeed they are sometimes absurd, and even repellent, and we are disgusted by Gulliver's exaggerated devotion to them. The dispassionate arguments of the assembly, for instance, about the nature and future fate of Gulliver and the Yahoos, show the characteristic and unpleasant coldness of the Houyhnhnm race; while Gulliver's master displays their equally characteristic self-satisfaction, carried here to the point of absurdity, when he criticizes Gulliver's physical qualities. Gulliver tells us how his master interrupted his account of the relations of the European Yahoos with their horses, to point out the inferiority for all practical purposes of the Yahoo shape – 'the Flatness of my Face, the Prominence of my Nose, mine Eyes placed directly in Front, so that I could not look on either Side without turning my Head; that I was not able to feed myself without lifting one of my fore Feet and my Mouth; and therefore Nature had placed those Joints to answer that Necessity'. Throughout the book there are obvious blunders which cannot be explained away by the inevitable lack of positive attraction in rational Utopias. One of Swift's most attractive characters Don Pedro de Mendez, is placed in a position at the end of the book where comparison with the Houyhnhnms is inevitable, and our sympathies are alienated by the humourless arrogance both of the Houyhnhnms themselves, and of Gulliver when, absorbed in admiration of his former master, he avoids his family to concentrate on 'neighing of those two degenerate Houyhnhnms I keep in my Stable'. Clumsiness of this kind is not usual with Swift, who is well aware, as a rule, of the way to enlist our sympathy for a character, and shews his awareness in the drawing of M. B. Drapier, and of Gulliver in the Voyage to Lilliput. The whole course of his work makes it unlikely that he could be unaware of the unpleasantness of such passages as these. Possibly, then, the effect is a deliberate one, and the Houyhnhnms, far from being a model of perfection, are intended to show the inadequacy of the life of reason. This would be in keeping with the usual method of Swift's satire, and with the negative quality which has been observed in it. The characteristic of Swift's satire is precisely his inability, or his refusal to present us straightforwardly with a positive to aim at. It may be, at bottom, a psychological or a spiritual weakness; he turns it to satiric strength, and produces satire which is comfortless but is also disturbing and courageous. He will leave us with nothing more than a few scattered hints of what is desirable and attainable, or sometimes, when what is desirable is clearly not to be had, with a half-ironic acceptance of the best that is to hand. A full, clear, and wholly unambiguous account of a state of life to aim at would be unusual and unexpected in Swift. It is his habit to look sceptically, not only at the evils of the world, but at those, including himself, who criticize such evils, and at those who present schemes for the betterment of mankind. Gulliver is quaintly indignant and surprised at the evils which still exist six months after the publication of his travels, and in *A Tale of a Tub* the Digression on Madness ends with a confession which undermines the whole: 'Even I myself, the Author of these Momentous Truths, am a person whose Imaginations are hardmouth'd, and exceedingly Disposed to run away with his Reason.' In fact, there is not usually a 'norm' in Swift's satire, positively and unequivocally stated. As far as any positive position can be discovered, it must be by piecing together the hints and implications and indirections typical of Swift's whole method; it is foreign to that method to embody in one person or one race a state of things of which he fully approves. It is, indeed, more than a matter of satiric method for a man 'betwixt two Ages cast', who had little of which he could approve wholeheartedly. The spirit of compromise and common sense, the love of the middle way, affected him sufficiently to undermine any more rigorous standards, while failing to satisfy him as it satisfied his younger contemporaries; and his position was further complicated by a strong feeling for existing forms and a dislike of innovation, which, like Dryden, he regards as dangerous. Any suggestion of radical remedies is distrusted by him even as he presents it and he will withdraw from it into irony, or fall back into compromise as he does in the ambiguous *Argument against Abolishing Christianity*.

In Gulliver's Travels, this characteristic method re-appears. In the first two books, no one person or group of persons is put forward for our approval, and neither the Lilliputians, the Brobdingnagians, nor Gulliver himself, can be regarded as a consistent satiric norm against which the moral and political vagaries of eighteenth-century England are to be precisely measured. Swift slips from one side to another according as his isolated satiric points require it, and we are at one moment to admire, at another to dislike, the creatures of his imagination. Even in Laputa, a set of serious political schemes, such as the visionary project of 'persuading Monarchs to chuse Favourites upon the Score of their Wisdom, Capacity and Virtue', appears among the absurdities of the projectors. Gulliver himself is now honest and kindly, now credulous or pompous, according to the momentary demands of the satire. During his adventures in Brobdingnag he is frequently ridiculous and on one occasion definitely unpleasant; his complacent attitude to warfare, in chapter

VI, horrifies the giant King. In none of the first three books are we left with a consistent standard embodied in any creature; and it would seem that if the Houyhnhnms are presented fairly and squarely for our approval a change is involved not only in Swift's normal method but in his whole attitude of mind. He would hardly present the radical primitivism and rationalism of Houyhnhnm-land as desirable, at least without the ironic and sceptical withdrawal which his uncertain temperament demanded.

One would expect to find that Swift uses the Houyhnhnms in the same indirect way as he does the peoples of the earlier books, not as a complete statement of the right kind of man or society, attainable or not, but as a satiric contrast in which good and less good are mixed in proportion which we must decide for ourselves, with the aid of such hints of the author's as we can piece together. And in fact Swift is just as ready to sacrifice the consistency of the Houyhnhnms to their satiric function of innocent comment on unknown humanity as he is any of his other creatures. The opinion of Gulliver's master on the 'prodigious Abilities of Mind' of English lawyers, which should qualify them to instruct others in wisdom and knowledge, leads to a valid satiric point, but does not show the Houyhnhnm in a very good light when one considers the damning account he has just heard of their moral depravity and lack of intellectual integrity. No doubt one reason why the Houyhnhnms are a race of animals is for satiric distance; but of course Swift's insistence on the animal in Book IV has a significance beyond that of satiric effectiveness. Several of the Houyhnhnms' characteristics seem to be intended to show their remoteness, and their irrelevance to the ordinary life and standards of mankind. Primitivism is used for this effect; they have great difficulty in understanding such humanly simple matters as Gulliver's clothes, his ship, his writing, and the Houyhnhnms in his dealings with Gulliver in chapter III is not only unattractive, but unattractive in a particular way. 'He brought me into all Company,' Gulliver says of him, 'and made them treat me with Civility because as he told them privately, this would put me into good Humour and make me more diverting.' This may be intended to lessen Gulliver's status and lower his pride, but Swift could hardly have missed its effect of displaying the lack of humanity and sympathy, the cold curiosity of the Houyhnhnms. There is, too, the solemn criticism of Gulliver's physical characteristics in chapter IV, part of which has already been quoted. This passage stresses the fact that man is not well endowed, either physically or mentally, to live a 'natural' life; but it also shows the Houyhnhnm's inability to grasp the human point of view, his self-righteousness, and his determination to belittle these creatures who in their own land claim to rule over the Houyhnhnm race. The Houyhnhnms are alien and unsympathetic creatures, not man at his best, as Godwin suggested, or man as he might be, but a kind of life with which humanity has nothing to do. The word Houyhnhnm, we are told, means 'Perfection of Nature'. These are not human beings, but virtuous animals, perfect but limited natural creatures, of a 'nature' not simply unattainable by man, but irrelevant to him, and incapable not simply unattainable by man, but irrelevant to him, and incapable not only of the depths, but also of the heights, to which humanity can reach. The Houyhnhnms have no shame, no temptations, no conception of sin: they are totally unable to comprehend the purpose of lying or other common temptations of man. They can live by reason because they have been created passionless. In man, we know, the passions are apt to get astride of the reason, which is not strong enough to restrain them, and the result in its extremest form is seen in the Yahoos, but the Houyhnhnms have no passions to control: 'As these noble Houyhnhnms are endowed by Nature with a general Disposition to all Virtues, and have no Conceptions or Ideas of what is evil in a rational creature, so their grant Maxim is, to cultivate Reason, and to be wholly governed by it.' The point of the description lies in 'as' and 'so'. The Houyhnhnms can live harmlessly by reason because their nature is different from ours.

Swift makes much of the differing natures of Houyhnhnms, the Yahoos, and Gulliver himself. In the Houyhnhnms, nature and reason are one and the same. They have no 'natural affections' in our sense; Nature, they say, has taught them to be equally benevolent to everyone, and to make a distinction of persons only on the rational grounds of 'a superior Degree of Virtue'. Marriage is undertaken simply as 'one of the necessary Actions in a reasonable Being'. Nor have they any fear of death, which they greet with the same complete absence of emotion that they show towards every other event, great or small. These attitudes are not those which Nature teaches human beings, as Swift recognizes both in *Gulliver's Travels* and elsewhere; man has affections and passions, and Swift seems not to regard them as wholly bad. The painful and universal fear of death in mankind was a subject which particularly interested and affected him, and the curious episode of the immortal Struldbrugs in the third Voyage is an attempt to deal with it. Gulliver wished to take some of the Struldbrugs back with him to England, 'to arm our People against the Fear of Death', that dread which Nature has implanted in us, but not in the Houyhnhnms. In the *Thoughts on Religion* reason is brought to bear on the problem: 'It is impossible that anything so natural, so necessary, and so universal as death, should ever have been designed by providence as an evil to mankind.' But reason is powerless against man's fear of death, and his clinging to life on any terms; and Swift puts forward the idea that although in general reason was intended by Providence to govern our passions, in this God intended our passions to prevail over reason. Man cannot in all respect govern his passions by reason, he suggests, because he has not been equipped by Providence to do so; perhaps both love of life and the propagation of the species are passions exempted by Providence, for particular purposes, from the control of reason. The precise amount of irony in such statements is always difficult to gauge, though the *Thoughts on Religion* are not satirically intended; but at least the passage shows Swift's feeling that such deep-rooted passions as these are part of the nature of man, created by God, and cannot and perhaps should not be ruled by reason. The Houyhnhnms are rational even in those things in which the wisest man's passions inevitably and even perhaps rightly rule him, and the handling of them seems to suggest not only the remoteness but the inadequacy by human standards, of the life of Reason. They have only the negative virtue of blamelessness.

The Houyhnhnms refer repeatedly to Gulliver's fellow-humans in terms which press home the contrast between themselves and mankind. Men are creatures 'pretending to Reason', the character of a rational creature was one which mankind 'had no Pretence to challenge'. Again the Houyhnhnms thought that 'Nature and Reason were sufficient Guides for a reasonable Animal, as we pretended to be'. Man has no right to lay claim to the life of Reason, for in him nature and reason are not, as in the Houyhnhnms, identical, and there is that in his nature which is outside reason's legitimate control. But this is not necessarily to say that man's nature is thoroughly evil, and his situation hopeless, as in the case of the degenerate Yahoos, nor is man treated in these terms. Gulliver and the other humans of Book IV are clearly distinguished from the Yahoos as well as from the Houyhnhnms, and the difference in their mental and physical habits is strongly insisted upon. They stand apart from the two races of this animal world, separated from both by characteristics of which neither the naturally virtuous and rational animals, nor the vicious and irrational ones, have any knowledge — in fact by the characteristics proper to humanity. Man does indeed share the Yahoos' propensity to evil, but he has compensating qualities which the Bestial Yahoos have not possessed since their first degeneration; and with these qualities he may surpass the cold rational virtue of the Houyhnhnms. The member of that race who is treated with most sympathy by Swift is the humble sorrel nag, one of the servant breeds who were 'not born with equal Talents of Mind.' Into the incompletely rational mind of the nag, some near-human warmth and devotion can creep, and he is the only creature in Houyhnhnm-land to show any affection; Gulliver's last link with the country as he sails away is the voice of the 'Sorrel Nag (who always loved me) crying out..... Take Care of thyself, gentle Yahoo.'

With this partial exception, there is no sign among the Houyhnhnms of kindness, compassion, or self-sacrifice, yet elsewhere in *Gulliver's Travels* there is sympathetic treatment of love, pity, and a deliberate intervention of one man in the life of another, very different from the Houyhnhnm's equal benevolence, detachment, and rational respect for virtue. Even in Book I, where moral satire is not at its most serious, there is an insistence on the importance of gratitude among the Lilliputians, by whom, we are told in chapter VI, ingratitude is regarded as a capital crime. Gratitude is shown in action in Gulliver's behaviour to the Lilliputian King, when despite the King's unjust sentence upon him he cannot bring himself to retaliate, for, he tells us, 'Neither had I so soon learned the Gratitude of Courtiers, to persuade myself that his Majesty's present Severities quitted me of all past Obligations.'

In Book II there is the forbearance of the giant King and the affection between Gulliver and the protective Glumdalclitch, and in Book IV great prominence is given to the Captain and crew of the ship which rescues Gulliver. Swift makes it plain that the Portuguese sailors are admirable human beings, and emphasizes in them the very qualities which the Houyhnhnms neither possess nor would understand. It is Don Pedro who persuades Gulliver to abandon his design of living as a recluse, following as far as he can the life of a rational detached virtue which the Houyhnhnms have taught him to admire, and instead to commit himself once more to the human relationships proper to mankind. Gulliver's duty as Don Pedro sees it is to return to a life of humanity, tolerance and affection among his own people, and Gulliver, finding he can do no better, reluctantly agrees. But his behaviour towards his own family, set in a place where it contrasts forcibly with the tolerant practical goodwill of Don Pedro, is exaggerated to the point of madness. Only with difficulty can he endure the sight of the wife and children for whom he had shown so charming a fondness in the past. Gulliver, once a normal affectionate human, concerned with the well-being of his friends, is now a solitary misanthrope, absurd and yet terrible in his self-concentration and his loathing of those he had once loved. He had been, he tells us, a great lover of mankind, and his conduct in the previous voyages shows that he was particularly affectionate to his own family. Now they 'dare not presume to touch my Bread, or drink out of the same Cup'. To this point Gulliver has been led by his pride in the unaided reason. He has become inhuman, losing the specifically human virtues in his attempt to achieve something for which humanity is not fitted. He is ruined as a human being, and the failure of his fellows to attain his own alien standards has made him hate them. We are reminded of Swift's letter (26 November 1725) to Pope: 'I tell you after all, that I do not hate mankind: it is "vous autres", who hate them, because you would have them reasonable animals, and are angry for being disappointed.' Gulliver is one of 'vous autres', for to set for humanity the irrelevant standards of absolute reason is to end as Gulliver ended, in hatred and defect. Swift was well aware of the process of disillusionment which has been attributed to him, and he exemplifies it in Gulliver, the true misanthrope, who believes man should try to rule himself by 'Reason alone'.

On this interpretation, neither the master Houyhnhnm nor the misanthropic Gulliver who once thought so highly of mankind is presented as an ideal of behaviour. Like all the people of the *Travels* the Houyhnhnms have some characteristics, such as honesty and truthfulness, which we might well try to follow, and they are used for particular satiric points, but as a whole they represent an inadequate and inhuman rationalism, and the negativeness of their blameless life is part of Swift's deliberate intention. For us, with our less perfect but also less limited nature, to try to live like them would be to do as the Stoics did, according to Swift's remark in his *Thoughts on Various Subjects*: 'The Stoical Scheme of Supplying our Wants by lopping off our Desires, is like cutting off our Feet when we want shoes.' It would mean abandoning the purely human possibilities as well as the disadvantages of our own nature. The Houyhnhnms may indeed be compared with the passionless Stoics of the sermon 'Upon the Excellency of Christianity', who are contrasted with the Christian ideal of positive charity. Gulliver, in his turn, shows the loss of hope, proportion, and even common humanity in a man who tries to limit the complex nature of man to 'Reason alone'. Something more than Houyhnhnm harmlessness is needed in a world of human beings, and in so far as there is any positive presentation of right living to be found in *Gulliver's Travels*, it is in the representatives of that humanity which Gulliver rejects. For it is not, after all, a purely destructive view of humanity that Swift shows us. 'Reason and Nature' indeed are set up only to be shown as inadequate. Swift never doubted that man should make use of reason to control his bad instincts where he can, but to live by reason alone is neither possible nor desirable if we are to remain human beings. Yet we have the generous King of Brobdingnag, whose people are the 'least corrupted' of Yahoos or humans, and of whom Swift says, with his habitual indirection, 'it would be hard indeed, if so remote a Prince's Notion of Virtue and Vice were to be offered as a Standard for all Mankind'. And there is Don Pedro de Mendez, who shows to what unselfish goodness man can attain. Don Pedro is guided by 'Honour and Conscience', and for Swift, as we know from the sermons, conscience was not a natural sense of right and wrong or Shaftesbury's 'aesthetic perception of the harmony of the universe', but a faculty which must itself be guided by the divine laws which we can know only from a source outside ourselves, from revelation. 'There is no solid, firm Foundation for Virtue' – he tells us in the sermon 'On the Testimony of Conscience' – 'but on a Conscience which is guided by Religion.' 'There is no other Tie thro' which the Pride, or Lust, or Avarice, or Ambition of Mankind will not certainly break one time or other.' For him, as far so many Churchmen concerned with the controversies of the period, Reason is an insufficient guide without Revelation. The sermons, with their systemic attack on the supposed sufficiency of the moral sense, the scheme of virtue without religion, are clearly relevant to the theme of the fourth Voyage of *Gulliver's Travels* and here we find the positive aspect of Swift's intention more explicitly set out. The sermon 'Upon the Excellency of Christianity' shows, in its account of the ideal Christian, a creature who is meek and lowly, 'affable and courteous, gentle and kind, without any morose leaven of pride or vanity, which entered into the composition of most Heathen schemes.' The description applies far more nearly to Don Pedro and the early Gulliver than to the Houyhnhnms, or to Gulliver the misanthrope into whose composition pride certainly enters. While allowing a place to the passions and affections, and their possibility, under guidance, for good, Swift does not fall into the Tillotsonian position that human nature's mild and merciful' inclinations and the maternal and other natural affections are more important than revealed religion. An implied disapproval of such a position is expressed in Swift's version of Anthony Collins' *Discourse of Freethinking*, in which Tillotson, naturally, is praised. Both affections and reason have their place in the well-regulated man, but they are to be subjected to the laws of God. Reason and gratitude may both suggest to a man that he should obey his parents, but the surest and most lasting cause of obedience must be the consideration 'that his Reason is the Gift of God; that God commanded him to be obedient to the Laws, and did moreover in a particular manner enjoin him to be Dutiful to his Parents' ('On the Testimony of Conscience'), Swift would no doubt have agreed with that passage from Butler's sermon 'Upon Compassion' (published in the same year as *Gulliver's Travels*) in which passions and affections, carefully guided, are treated as necessary in creatures who are imperfect and interdependent, 'who naturally and, from the condition we are placed in, necessarily depend upon each other. With respect to such creatures, it would be found of as bad consequence to eradicate all natural affections, as to be entirely governed by them. This would almost sink us to the condition of brutes; and that would leave us without a sufficient principle of action.' The passage forms a comment on the contrasting creatures of Houyhnhnm-land, for Swift is as well aware as Butler of the complex nature of man, the professor not only of evil impulses but of passions and affections which under the guidance of conscience and religion (to which reason must be subject) can issue in virtuous action, especially that compassionate assistance to our fellow men, whether or not our reason judges them worthy of it, which 'the Gentile philosophy' fails to produce. In *Gulliver's Travels* there is only a traditional Christian pessimism; there may well be a positive Christian ideal suggested in the conduct of the good humans, though it is presented with Swift's habitual obliquity and restraint.

From *Swift: Modern Judgements*. Ed. Norman A. Jeffares (London: Macmillan and Co Ltd), 1968.

TOPICS FOR DISCUSSION

1. *Gulliver's Travels* can be primarily read as a tale of adventure. Substantiate this tracing the course of the novel.
2. If *Gulliver's Travels* is just a travel book, it covers certain fictitious places. How will you read it in terms of travel literature for the adult reader?
3. *Gulliver's Travels* actually moves beyond travel and adventure to make statements on human life and passes judgments on different aspects of so-called civilised life. How would you examine the book in this light? Discuss.
4. Swift has written a satirical study of human nature, human politics and government. Use examples from the book to illustrate this statement.
5. Some critics read the book as an allegory of life. Explore this aspect of *Gulliver's Travels.*

6. There is no strict plot in *Gulliver's Travels* as it is episodic in nature. How will you substantiate this statement?
7. Discuss Book II: 'A Voyage to Brobdingnag', as a commentary on power and its abuses in society.
8. How does Book III: 'A Voyage to Laputa, Balnibari, Glubbubdrib, Luggnagg and Japan' become a satire on science and its advancement?
9. Discuss Gulliver's experiments in the land of the Yahoos. Why does he dislike being called a Yahoo?
10. Is the land of the Houyhnhnms an ideal society and a 'rational Utopia'? Discuss.
11. Do you think that Swift is offering a comment on master-subordinate relationships in his portrayal of an Englishman as being subordinate to the monarchs of every land he finds himself in, even to a race of horses. Discuss.
12. Discuss *Gulliver's Travels* as an open assertion of Swift's disillusionment with the state of life in England.

FURTHER READING

Primary Sources

1. *A Tale of a Tub* (1704)
2. *The Battle of the Books* (1704)
3. *A Trip to Dunkirk, or A Hue and Cry after the Pretended Prince of Wales* (1708)
4. *Predictions for the year 1708; written to prevent the people of England from being further impos'd on by vulgar almanack-makers, by Isaac Bickerstaff, Esq.* (1708)
5. *The Accomplishment of the First of Mr. Bickerstaff's Predictions: Being an Account of the Death of Mr. Partridge, the almanack-maker* (1708)
6. *A Grub Street Elegy, on the Supposed Death of Mr. Partridge, the Almanack-Maker* (1708)
7. *Baucis and Philemon* (1708)
8. *An Argument against Abolishing Christianity in England* (1708)
9. *A Vindication of Isaac Bickerstaff, Esq.* (1709)

10. *Hints Towards an Essay on Conversation* (1709)
11. *A famous Prediction of Merlin, the British Wizard* (1709)
12. *A Letter concerning the Sacramental Test* (1709)
13. *A Project for the Advancement of Religion, and the Reformation of Manners* (1709)
14. *A Meditation upon a Broom-Stick* (1710)
15. *The Virtues of Sid Hamet the Magician's Rod* (1710)
16. *A Proposal for Correcting, Improving and Ascertaining the English Tongue* (1712)
17. *Some Advice Humbly Offer'd to the Members of the October Club* (1712)
18. *The Conduct of the Allies* (1712, pub. 1713)
19. *The Public Spirit of the Whigs* (1714)
20. *A Proposal for the Universal Use of Irish Manufactures* (1720)
21. *A Letter of Advice to a Young Poet* (1721)
22. *Gulliver's Travels* (1726)
23. *A Short View of the State of Ireland* (1727)
24. *An Account of the Empire of Japan* (1728)
25. *An Essay on Modern Education* (1728)
26. *A Modest Proposal* (1729)

Secondary Sources

Bloom, Harold. Ed. *Gulliver's Travels*. Delhi: Viva, 2003.

Donoghue, Denis. Ed. *Jonathan Swift: A Critical Anthology*. Hamondsworth: Penguin, 1971

Gravil, Richard. Swift: *Gulliver's Travels: A Casebook*. London: Macmillan, 1974.

Nokes, David. *Jonathan Swift, A Hypocrite Reversed: A Critical Biography*. Oxford: Oxford Univ. Press, 1985.

Rawson, C. J. *Gulliver and the Gentle Reader: Studies in Swift and Out Time*. London: Routledge and Kegan Paul, 1973.

Tippett, Brian. *Gulliver's Travels: The Critics Debate*. Atlantic Highlands, N.J: Humanities Press, 1989.

Tuveson, Ernest. *Swift: A Collection of Critical Essays*. New Delhi: Prentice-Hall of India, 1979.

Voigt, Milton. *Swift and the Twentieth Century*. Detroit: Wayne State Univ. Press, 1964.